Following Hemingway to Paris

Following Hemingway to Paris

The Lighter Side of Depression and Alcohol-abuse in the City of Lights

Michael William Newman

iUniverse, Inc.
New York   Bloomington

Following Hemingway to Paris

The Lighter Side of Depression and Alcohol-abuse in the City of Lights

This is a work of fiction. All of the characters, names, incidents, organizations, and dialogue in this novel are either the products of the author's imagination or are used fictitiously.

iUniverse books may be ordered through booksellers or by contacting:

iUniverse
1663 Liberty Drive
Bloomington, IN 47403
www.iuniverse.com
1-800-Authors (1-800-288-4677)

ISBN: 978-1-4401-0463-3 (pbk)
ISBN: 978-1-4401-0464-0 (ebk)

Printed in the United States of America

iUniverse rev. date: 11/10/08

For Father

A child of suicide never forgets.

\- Kurt Vonnegut

Chapter I

I cannot say that I will, but if I decide again to toss my life – the job, close contacts with friends and family, known-comforts, season tickets to the Redskins - and take Julia and our two babies and march on towards newer and greener pastures, Paris would not be my next New Jerusalem. Why this contradiction with regards to my love of the City of Lights? I can explain without remorse: my love for Paris is sadly an unrequitted love- my wife, children, and I could spend our whole lives there and never be regarded as true Parisians.

The true Parisians, the *baguettes*, lead a double life. They are at the same time an insular community, deliberately isolated from what many see as the corrupting force of the longstanding, fickle, ex-pat community and the surrounding African and Muslim slums, and an integrated unindividualized part of European culture.

And despite the long standing allure, the City of Lights no longer can claim fame as the darling final destination of many young, wanton, ex-pat Americans. With its infant capitalist markets, cheap living, and individualized, undiluted cultures, Eastern and Central Europe are fast becoming the New Continent in stark contrast to France's Old Europe ideology and mixed society. Finance is a good barometer of the influence a country or region has on the young and savvy, and investing in Central Europe is the latest and greatest big bet for international players. These countries were soon glad candidates for joining the European Union and European Monetary Union. It is a quantum leap. Moreover, these countries, because of sheer political will and other internal pressures, are moving fast from their decrepit communist past to first world economies as far as hard currency and legal frameworks can take them. With the introduction of the Euro, the economies of the Czech Republic, Hungary, and Poland are due to boom and bloom with capitalism.

Yet I find that something is missing from these new, youthful destinations.

With an age approaching two millenia, Paris does contain much wisdom still to endow on the dream-seeker, including a veritable mix of enchanting cultural and social liberties surely not found anywhere else on this planet. The silver spoon and champagne set know no better place than Paris to traipse around, defying the poverties of the rest of the world.

A cup of coffee with cream anywhere in the world is just a drink. In Paris, *un cafe au lait* is an experience not to be missed.

In London or New York City, a man who expresses too much interest in his own attire is relegated to being a gay fop; in Paris, he is labelled no more than an average *citoyen*.

In New York City, art is cutting edge. In Milan, it is perennial. In Paris, it is both. In other metropolises people have unanswered dreams; in Paris, one has memories.

But living in Paris as a student (my first year in Paris) and working in Paris are not the same thing, and this was a crucial difference that led to my decision to leave the great city for the the reliable comforts of America. Transportation strikes happen all too regulary thus necessitating that the workers of the city hoof it to their jobs. Students rally and protest and block major thoroughfare with such energy that many call their demonstrations the national sport. And what can be said of the Socialists and their quest for more tax revenue? Julia and I gave nearly 65% of our meager wages to the government. The amount we paid out of our checks before the take home was so great that we had little left to spend on necessities, and high city prices for such goods are further exacerbated by France's 20% value added tax to any purchases. Yes, the Socialist government services are some of the best in the world and the World Health Organization puts France's medical care system at the top of its annual list year after year. But when a government and its services employ more than 40% of the population, as France's does, something is not right in a democracy. De Gaulle would not be pleased.

Sweden and Norway are considered by the United Nations to be the best places in Europe (and the world) to emigrate to. Denmark is rated the free-est country socially and politically according to the same U.N. report. Immigrants of African origin can be seen working in banks and offices in Great Britain. And now in Ireland, an African emigre was voted in as mayor of a small town. (It's true. His name is Rotimi Adebari; the town is Portlaoise, an hour outside of Dublin.) All that is to say, the rest of Europe is becoming more progressive socially, but France still stands out as a country with abject racial undertones. And nothing is being done about it.

Some people say that Paris is timeless and that it is on the verge of a comeback as the center of culture for the European Union. Even if Paris builds itself out of the hole the Socialist government has dug for itself by limiting services to non-Europeans, the amalgam of foreigners from Africa and elsewhere will continue further to color the city. And the True Parisian will continue to complain and weep at this thought. What else to offer, besides the populist Le Pen?

Julia and I were never accepted in Paris – our neighbors in the apartment across the way, who were noisy when they made love for everyone in the whole building to hear, never uttered a word when we crossed in the building stairs, despite Julia's and my verbal attempts to introduce ourselves on each occasion. And since we were then married and wanting to start a family, it was time to leave. *Paris and all of its enchantment are as ephemeral as the tulips in the Champs de Mars,* I said to Charlie the last time I spoke to him. *But the city will have to go on without us.*

Chapter II

Le Chat Noir is a bar-nightclub I often frequented between the metro stations Blanche and Pigalle in the center of Paris' famous red-light district, Pigalle. It is a great location to begin my story because unlike the other lesser known red-light district in Paris, Saint Denis, and most red-light districts around the world, Pigalle is a stone throw's distance to the second most famous Catholic basilica in Paris, Sacre Cœur. The first time I stood looking at both of these monoliths the stark irony was immediately apparent to the me. For as one who surely is a thinker and has always pondered the souls of men and their purpose, to see the great monument to the Holy Family rising above the illuminated porn shops and flesh palaces is to be able to finally understand in full a man's heart. To further add to the revelation, I can say that the visual and spiritual impact on a man's soul by one is not discounted by the other, especially when remembering that both were created by men.

Le Chat Noir itself is interesting because in no other large metropolis that I have visited exists a bar-nightclub with such darkened international feeling: where an insipid, English speaking North African immigrant serves Belgian white beer in liter mugs to gruff, blue-collar Frenchmen who come to listen to a black, dreadlock-wearing, Los Angeles native play American blues on the saxophone. The place can get as packed with people as the Saint Michel metro station during rush hour, but on Saturdays early in the evening before the blues band takes the stage the place is almost empty. My favorite time to frequent the bar was now, when the older, stodgier diners finish eating their *cote de vœu* and before the more hip and younger generation moves in to raise the roof in a joyous bacchanal celebration to nothing greater than God's gift of jazz music. At this time, around 8 pm to 10 pm to be more exact, I would find myself seated on a faded, faux leather circular bench, leaning back on a torn Lautrec-poster, talking to Olivier.

Many Parisians who enjoy a solitary vigil in a brasserie would disagree with me, but it is absurd to sit in a bar locale such as *Le Chat Noir* alone (I never did), and most, if not all, of the other customers there were heterosexual couples or groups of couples. And even though I was there as part of a heterosexual couple, since I never went to any social occasion in Paris without my Julia, sitting across from Olivier I learned to understand the importance of relationships between men. This was openly most apparent to Julia and whichever sister Olivier chose to bring with him because for most of the evening the two girls were not part of my and Olivier's deep discussions. Olivier and I made our choice, not the girls'. Our talks were profound, if not entirely philosophical – would there be any other way in the City of Lights? – and no subject was taboo, from even the moribund usuals, politics and religion, to more lively and self-actualizing topics, such as sex in the time of AIDS, and male competition in the urban environments. I smile now as I enthusiastically recall, to the best of my alcohol-impaired memory, these talks because at these times – solely and unforgivingly at these times – I forgot how lost and unimportant I was in the big city.

Pigalle would be nothing without the bright, neon lights of the porn establishments beckoning the street-wanderers to abandon the dark sidewalks of the Boulevard Clichy for a plausible evening of hedonism. (I am not completely sure whether the bright lights have anything to do with it, but I would wager that it is precisely because Pigalle is so brightly lit that it is one of the safer red-light districts in the world, even during the wee-est of hours.) The neon lights from the surrounding porn shops penetrated the windows of *Le Chat Noir* so strongly, and the interior lighting was so inadequate that Olivier and I were never quite able to see the expressions on one anothers' faces while we emotionally discussed the tales of men's souls. Given this failure of vision, and the dreadful language barriers (Olivier's slow English and my fractured, anglicanized French), misunderstandings were common. I remember on one slightly drunken occasion Olivier was speeking freely about the importance of persistence in pursuing 'a penis' while in the midst of the ephemeral moroseness of life. I was shocked and confused to hear him speak of homosexuality this way, of course, but he never knew it and kept on unabashedly with the same topic, occasionally pounding on the marble table-top and clinking his mug with mine to emphasize his conviction. Though funny to say now, it really took me damn near twenty-five minutes to realize he was saying 'happiness' and the not the word for the male organ.

I find it easy to say that our talks were usually limited to men's philosophical matters because we were so engrossed with ourselves. When on the rare occasion of mutual ennui we deigned to include Julia and Olivier's sister, the talk was more focussed on Paris' living standards, which I found an insufferably sterile subject in itself to discuss. Repeatedly, the girls' main concerns were money, and, more specifically, how little money we all had, and concurrently the inflated cost of living in Paris over other parts of France. Paris was not cheap, is not a bargain, and would always be expensive, I would expound to them in exasperation, as divine inspiration is costly. And it was true, even for fortunate me with my American patrimony and with the almighty dollar at historical highs when compared to the Euro.

But I felt this so deleterious to speak about that when the girls took over the conversation I took to my drink. White beer in a liter mug became the better part of many of my evenings' fare. Alcohol was integral to enjoying myself out. For my sake, beer and wine were listed first by Julia on our entertainment budget (though I viewed them as essentials), with nothing else really noted after. For Julia, the alcohol was a waste of money – she preferred to spend our hard-earned Euro on cabaret shows and American films on the Champs-Elysees, and on the occasional late-evenings of dancing in Paris discotheques. She did not appreciate alcohol. I really enjoyed drinking to an almost excess while in Paris, especially early in the evening, either in my home or at places such as *Le Chat Noir*. After an early introduction by Olivier to red Bordeaux wine and Belgian beer, alcohol quickly became a part of my Paris life, and I looked forward to the opportunity to partake in it with all who would join me. I enjoyed it not like an addict who craves a fix in bodily desperation, but like an athlete who appreciates the physical high as part of his accomplishment. I was only just beginning to be an intellectual at the late age of 34 and alcohol, with its high, was a welcome complement. The god-awful problem was that even though the Hoogaarden beer I drank at *Le Chat Noir* was good, were it not for the conversations with Olivier (and the blues music), spending six Euro, twenty for a medium mug just would not have been justifiable. It took a few mugs to get boiled - I am even suspicious that the draught beer was watered down somewhere between the barrels in the basement and the spout at the bar - so the beer flowed well and easily across the zinc bar, and my money flowed in the other direction. Still, the chance to meet regularly and discuss life with a good friend more than made up for my literally pissing away a hard earned salary.

For his part, Olivier would never admit it, but he made a sizeable salary as a consultant in the energy industry and thus for him alcohol was not an expensive extra like it was for me. Eight and a half Euro for a Mojitos cocktail while dancing at the Cuba Cafe was not a waste for him, and three an evening was not unusual. His drinking was a 'natural part of the pleasure in living', he said, and which is still an outstanding curiosity for me given his Muslim heritage. Still his enjoyment was comforting to me; I was glad he drank so much – I would have been uncomfortable sitting with him in *Le Chat Noir* if he drank juice. I doubt I could have enjoyed my mug of beer if he did.

The music, the beer, and Olivier all made for many grand *soirees* at *Le Chat Noir*. As my good fortune would have it, *Le Chat Noir* was popular with the Frenchies and virtually unknown to tourists. You can ask any recent tourist to Paris for a good place for a social evening in Pigalle and he will invariable mention *Le Moulin Rouge* or *Les Folies Bergers*, the world famous cabarets with dancing women in red, frumpy skirts with no tops. But only the true Frenchies, the *baguettes* as my brother called them, know where and how to enjoy a drink and listen to some fine, live music.

I have read about and heard about and visited a plethora of legendary social-gathering places in Paris and each of them is arguably the quaintest, the liveliest, the most artistically and philosophically inspiring. But I liked *Le Chat Noir* best because, despite my arrogant, grossly exaggerated misbeliefs about my personal intellectual advancement while in Paris, there I made flowery recollections of the simple beauty of the loving people in my life, and there, in my brain's numbing alcoholic haze, I forgot how much of my life was wasted in debilitating clinical depression.

Chapter III

I had had a good and spirit-filled three Summer months in Paris when I first began to feel deep in my soul that the days were getting considerably darker and shorter. Autumn in northern France comes early and heavily, without remorse, bringing longer shadows, colder, dryer air, and more frequent rain. Each is individually soul-searingly painful for me to bear – the rain alone would make a solitary Londoner long for home - and when combined the abject desire to hibernate engulfed me then, as it does each year, but even more unrelentingly. For many weekends between Labor Day and Easter I spent the larger part of my waking hours, which were fewer than the lighter seasons, under thick blankets plastered to my warm bed sleeping long hours or reading and rereading familiar passages in the Bible. The lack of motivation to do *anything* scared me into wasting hours pursuing spiritual enhancement, which I vainly hoped would save my tortured mind – tormented even further by the guilt of not getting up, going out, and enjoying Paris while I had the chance. I had left the comforts of a good job, close family and friends, and a stable environment in Washington, DC for just that chance to take advantage of all the City of Lights has to offer. I really had the greatest opportunity to feed and grow my late-blossoming intellectual side, but I squandered it in my untreated clinical depression.

My Julia was worlds beyond anyone I have ever known in giving me comfort and understanding during this painful period. She was a tower of serenity without fail. I cannot count the number of times I was unjustly short of temper with her and she patiently held a high countenance. She would sit calmly on the edge of the the bed and listen to my verbal inanities, nodding silently, as only to acknowledge that I hurt.

Whenever I asked, and many times when I did not, she took time out from cleaning the flat and preparing our meals to bring me *verveine* with honey and lie with me for awhile. These are some of the most pleasurable memories I have of my time in Paris: just making love with my Julia in our quiet apartment, in a quiet building, on a quiet street, in a quiet quarter of Paris - in our chosen solitude. Her glowing face in front of mine – her eyes glistening. Her soft body radiating warmth underneath me, both of us under the bristly blankets. The perfumed smell of her clean hair. Her silky, Latina skin slowly brushing against my body. Sensual hours passed as seconds as we caressed, loved, and shared our bodies with each other in our bed.

And though I believe it always and for everyone to be possible to do so – man does have free will to choose his mate, you know - I would not have traded those times with Julia for anything or anyone else the world has to offer. Even God himself could not have given me more reason to live. Being alone and sexual with my Julia at that time of my life did not fulfill me with the same physical ecstasy that I had experienced during the sex of my teenage years – not the great novelty I remembered it to be - but it was everytime most pleasurable enough to perk up my soul, to instill a small amount of life in me, to make me smile when I just did not want to.

'*Pequena*?' That's what I called her – it means 'little one' in Spanish. '*Pequena*?' I asked her one chilly, rainy December Sunday after we had just finished making love. Her head laid across my bare chest.

'Yes, Meeko?' That's how she sounds with her accent as she says my name - and I never fail to grin when she says it.

I sighed. 'How can you make love to me when I am so edgy and unfulfilling to be around?'

She lifted her head. 'You really think you make difficult for me?'

'Yeah,' I forced a short laugh. 'I do.'

'Ah, Meeko. You know, to be with you and only you, it is so easy to do for me,' she replied with a sweetness in her Latina accent I cannot describe in words. 'You are very *especial* for me. Very, very *especial* for me. Never was someone *especial* for me like you.'

'Yes, I-,' I wanted to speak but she rolled over and pressed a finger to my lips.

She paused a moment then spoke. 'Meeko. Let me tell you something. Can I tell you something?' She leaned on one elbow, and slid her free hand across my forehead and stroked my hair as I continued to lay on my back.

'Ok,' I uttered, curious as to what she was going to say. I pivoted my head to look into her eyes. I always enjoyed Julia's little lectures directed at my obvious ignorance. And though there were many, and she spoke them often when I had almost no patience, I listened to each one carefully. She never did scold me; she only wished to help. She was careful only to use her words – her sometimes painfully limited vocabulary - to build me and other people up, and I knew that. Listening to her speak made me feel so warm inside, like I was again a young child comforted in the arms of my mother. Now, I waited for her to speak.

'I will tell you. The problems in your mind you have are little when are compared to my love for you. Why do you think of the problems? Do not think of the problems. You no careful, the problems will control. I will tell you, there will always be problems. But they are little; our love is bigger. Much more bigger. And the love is most important always. There will be always problems for us – this I know. You like to read your Genesis in your Bible, *no*?'

I nodded.

'You read even this Adam and Eve have problems. And it all begins so simply. Eve eats the apple and gives to Adam. And what happens?'

'It brought them death?' I offered. 'And as for death, all I think about these days is my father's suicide.'

'I know you do. But you see, you are wrong. Adam and Eve were already going to die. The apple was knowledge. Adam and Eve learned the knowledge of their future death and they must to live with this knowledge. But the problem of death exists before they know it. You see then, the problems were even before Adam and Eve were. This is your problem: your father's suicide. This, your father's death, is the knowledge you must to live with.'

I thought for a moment, then nodded to her with a crease in my eyebrows.

She smiled with a glint in her eye. 'Ah, Meeko. You must to know and I must to tell you that you cannot escape this knowledge, this death. This death of your poppy makes you afraid. You can try, but you cannot take this fear away. Like all men, you are afraid of the death like your father.'

'Actually,' I interrupted, 'I think I fear the stroke of death rather than death itself.'

'This does not matter. I tell you the love is perfect always and everywhere. Love pushes the fear away. Pushes it far, far away.'

'I don't see that happening. But then, nobody's ever told me what love is.'

'No one teach Adam and Eve to love-'

'So their love for each other is innate?' I asked rhetorically.

She arched her back. 'This I think.'

I laughed. 'You don't even know what the word innate means.'

She pointed a finger at me sternly. 'Stop to joke and listen! I tell you that you cannot read about the love Adam has for Eve in your Bible because it is not there in the words. It is not even mentioned, but is it not the most important, Adam and Eve's love for each other? Only the problems are written in your Bible: the problems of Adam, and his wife, and his children, and his children's children. The deaths- you read and you see the problems without solutions. This is for what I do not read your Bible. Put away your Bible. You must to focus on the love. And I love you, *pimpos*. Never I loved someone much I love you. We will be together always. This I promise you. And everywhere in the world we will be together always, *no*?'

I nodded shyly.

'You know, when I don't sometimes see you in the day I feel pain in my heart. Right here.' She put my hand on her warm breast. 'It is pain I can not explain easy for you. When you are at your teaching job and I am in the hair salon in the week and we are not together I have this pain in my heart. We are alonely then. But now here we are not alonely, yes? Because now we are together again to love. When we are together again the pain is not in my heart. Are you understanding me? I do not want to be alonely. Without you I still be alonely. Are you understanding me?'

I said nothing.

'I just love you, *pimpos*. So much. So, so much. And I want you to be as happy you make me. Please let me to make you happy.'

I could say nothing in reply; I only smiled weakly. It would have been so easy to cry, something I was always afraid to do in front of my Julia.

She looked concerned. 'Are you understanding me?' The steadiness of her gaze made me feel so accepted. The bedside lamp reflected in her deep, exotic eyes.

'Yes. I understand.' I exhaled softly, tilting my head back. 'You love me – even if I don't love myself.'

'Stop to judge yourself. It is not fair. It is not right. You confuse your emotions with the love. The two are not same.'

'And I need to forget about my father's suicide because thinking has no solution in itself, and no possible actions present themselves. And my emotional and drinking problems come from this. So you say. To feel better, I need only to focus on the love, right?'

'Mmmm, *si*, my *pimpos-pimpos*. Even if the emotions problems are always there, try to focus on the love. My love for you. Love is not emotion. Do not confuse them. Love is the body of God.'

She lowered her head to mine and we met with a long kiss, her hand gently sliding down my body.

The times in Paris we were together but not in bed, too, were love-filled and passionate. And my spirit wilted each time she got up and left me after our lovemaking – each time it felt as if we were in a boy loses girl novel – and I longed for the next time to be so close to that warm, soft body so full of compassion and serenity.

It was a great time to be in love with someone so *especial*.

Chapter IV

By the grace of God and the forgiveness of Prozac, not all of the fall and wintry days in Paris were so difficult to bear that I remained indoors. Some became quite enjoyable when I had the rare inspiration to get up and get out - to venture out with my Julia and walk the old, cobblestone streets of the Latin Quarter, Les Halles, and the Marais, snacking on a *crepe au chocolat*, drinking hot, spiced wine, and popping into used-book dealers.

We never chose to entertain others on our romantic city walks, even when relatives were in town. It was our time for each other. Just my Julia and *moi*. We chose to be alone – in our solitude – and the feelings for each other grew even stronger when we were in public. We remarked on no other passing persons in the streets, and surely no other streetwalker took the time to remark on us. Us - an American and a Latina - as inconspicuous as all the other foreign nationals coagulating in the world's most infamous melting pot.

We would begin our clandestine affairs by meeting at some romantic location – the fountain at Saint Michel was a favorite of Julia's; the Pompidou Center was mine - early on Saturday afternoons after my Julia finished her work at the salon. Each time she met me she was exhausted, having worked six days straight with Friday and Saturday the busiest. But she never let on to her fatigue; not a single unladylike complaint was ever uttered. Even more so, Julia left the work to me to map the perfect Parisian adventure to bring her back to life, complete with the requisite *Kir Royale* cocktails and *prix fixe* meal at a suprise location. Each walk we enjoyed was like the city streets and monuments we passed: each unique and beautiful, but nothing if separated from the whole experience of being there together. Being together was the most important part, for the most memorable walks, I recall, were not the longest, but the ones when we shared our souls' deepest longings with each other.

One Saturday mid-October there was a heavy fog – the *brouillard* as the French call it – all across Paris when I got off the 84 bus in front of the Pantheon, just off the Boulevard Saint Michel. I checked my watch – 1:40. I was quite early to meet my Julia, and because I had slept late and missed breakfast I stopped to munch on a *jambon* sandwich at a greasy joint – the kind of place one would not dare to take the mother-in-law to – and to read the International Herald Tribune. Though reading the screed was usually enjoyment enough for me, to complement my leisurely lunch this Saturday necessitated a *cafe au lait* and some pleasant conversation, both of which the brusque, unshaven North African man behind the counter was unable to provide.

'This not a cafe. You want *cafe au lait*, go to a cafe. Three Euro, twenty the sandwich,' he said gruffly.

His rejection and the Arabic music screeching on the radio at the top-strength of its dying batteries was enough to make me to want to slip back to the foggy boulevard as quietly as a freshman altar boy on Christmas Eve. I pulled four Euro in coins from my pocket and placed them gingerly on the counter. I smiled goodnaturedly as the North African turned again to look at me. The smile was not returned as he swiped the graphite counter with his dirty hands to pick up the money quickly, and, me, a little saddened, I picked up my newspaper to leave.

The North African drew a tip saucer from under the counter with some small clinking coins – my change. I waved a hand nonchalantly and wreaked a smile again.

'You not from France?' he asked, his eyebrows raised.

I replied that I was not.

He held up the few coins. 'Is why you 'ave a good heart,' he said with a toothless smile.

'Thank you,' I said meekly as I took a step towards the door.

'*Allaheismarladik.*'

'Excuse me?' I questioned.

'Allaheismarladik. Is Turkish. Means *go with Allah.*'

Oh, the portly man is Turkish, I learned, not North African.

'*Allaheismarladik,*' I struggled to repeat.

Still showing a toothless smile, he raised his hand holding the change, and made a short, deferential bow. I halted my step to return a bow in kind. A thin boy with oily hair brought a stack of dirty plates to the counter and he and my newfound Turkish friend began to speak, forgetting I was there.

And so I turned on my heel and walked out to the busy, foggy boulevard, my spirit barely lifted higher than the gutter at my feet, with a half-eaten ham sandwich in my pocket, to walk toward the Luxembourg Gardens and search for just the right cafe-spot to drink a *cafe au lait* and pass the hours before meeting my Julia. Couples both young and old were walking down the Boulevard Saint Michel arm in arm - some slowly, some briskly, all talking gaily without notice to the afternoon greyness or anyone else passing by. It all seemed so choreographed, the couples marching around not bumping into one another.

In the mid-afternoon darkness and quiet my thoughts carried me to my unredeeming preoccupation with that certain, inalienable question: *what is truth?* A question - I had come to the conclusion - probably not dared to be asked out loud by many great men in history, for fear of public reprisal, but surely screamed in their minds when they, like all of us inevitably, stood before their own mortal abyss. Pontius Pilate, for one, did dare to ask this question when Jesus stood before him- Jesus fully knowing and awaiting his condemnation. The first time I explored a literary (rather than dogmatic) perspective of this short scene in the Gospel of John, I found it impossible to forget – or rationalize. Did Pilate really want an answer? Or did he ask rhetorically? I do not know and the Bible fails to expound upon it. That *is* a serious problem I have with The Book: it leaves the reader and believer both hanging too much, too often. And as for Jesus, He just stood there silently, His head not raised. The reader knows: Jesus left Pilate hanging, too. Pilate never got an answer to his question in front of Jesus. In any manner, I took comfort in myself as I walked the cold and damp city knowing that I was not as scared to hell to think this question as I imagined Pilate surely was when he asked Jesus.

When I pushed open the door of the *Café Rostang* just across the Luxembourg Gardens, the lugubriousness of the quiet and gray life of the street I left behind me was erased by the enchantment of a bustling, however tenuous, environment. The air was dense with smoke, and with chatter such that I could not make out if the music in the background had any discernible vocals. Customers lined the bar three deep, and large groups of people crowded around the small marble tables. No place for me to grab a chair near the hustle of the bar, I pushed my way through the madding crowd to the portico and found a small iron table in front of the window in full view of the Gardens. A perfect corner to crash in for awhile, thanks be to the gods. Just after I took off my parka and hung it on the chair I stole from the next table, a carefully coiffed man in a black and white uniform stole place in front of me and asked me my order.

'*Cafe au lait*,' I replied, unnerved becuase I was not ready to have my order taken.

'No cafe, *m'sieu*,' he answered me.

'Okay, *une biere?*' I questioned. '*Pression.*'

'*Grande, m'sieu?*'

I sat down. '*Demi.*'

He raised his shoulders and turned his nose up sharply as if to say *very well, monsieur, make me go through that crowd for a lousy half-pint*. I could not help but to laugh. He grinned, nodded solemnly, and marched off.

I pulled a legal pad from my courior case – the one Julia gave me for my birthday to carry my class notes – and fingered a fountain pen from my parka. The desire to write came and went often during my time in Europe, but it was never consistent enough to entice me to create any truly substantive material over a long period of time. Mostly I wrote mini-sketches of different people, some of them my students, others friendly acquaintances who made an impact on my life in an uncommon sort of way. Usually I tore these writings to pieces a few weeks later having read them and condemned them as worthless. On occasion I typed up and photocopied some loose pages and brought them to the classes I taught for discussion, which was rarely useful in advancing my budding skill as a writer (students as harsh literary critics abound), but highly beneficial as a tool for teaching English.

I sat back, resting my pen on the pad, to take a relaxing breath and open my mind as one opens a bottle of fine bordeaux red to let it blossom, to let it *arrive* as the French say, for a time before drinking. Outside people were passing in the cold, indifferent to those of us inside the windows who watched them. We, who were so weak as to seek the false security of a warmer environment, watched all humanity pass us by.

'Oh, for the distilled tranquillity of my soul,' I exhaled.

'You think she's toast.'

I heard this, but was not paying attention.

'Fine, ignore me. But if you want I'll go tell her you think she's toast.'

I turned in my chair to eight o'clock. A slender, flinty girl with pink lipstick and matching blouse was leaning forward in a chair, one arm bent at the elbow locked on her legs crossed at the knee, and the other arm draped across the table in front of a half-empty highball glass. She twirled her shoulder-length brown hair nervously, feigning the appearance of ennui. When our eyes met she just blinked twice.

'Uh, hi,' I managed to force out.

She glanced down at her glass then back at me. 'You think she's toast, yes?'

'Who?'

'That one,' she said pointing out the window. 'Against the tree. You were staring straight at her.'

'Hadn't noticed.'

'She's toast. I know you were staring right at her. I know you guys want women like her.'

'And how do you get that?'

'The pouty lips, the blonde hair done up in a bun, rouge on the cheeks, that's all sexy. But she can't dress up right. Look at her leather pants. It's almost raining. It's December, and she's wearing leather pants. For gawd-sakes, only in Paris does a woman wear leather when it's raining in December. With those pumps she looks like a *putain*. Probably is, hiding in the daytime in the *Quartier Latin* away from her night job on her back in Pigalle.' She picked up her glass and took a swallow. 'I'll go tell her you say she's toast, if you want.'

'Not necessary. Not interested in *putes*,' I said.

21

'She may not be. I only said it's possible. She could just as well be a member of the Senate. The building's just down the street, you know, at the bottom of the Luxembourg Gardens.'

'A member of the French Senate.' I rolled my eyes. 'In leather pants. Standing and waiting in the drizzle. I can't bite on that piece of *fromage*.'

She gave me a quirky smile. 'Life is rife with contradictions. At social flummery, nobody tops our leaders in government.'

I was bemused by this. 'Do tell me,' I implored.

She placed a finger in her glass. 'You know, it is well known in France that leaders have affairs for sex, and money causes the scandal. But in the U.S. – where I guess you're from – people have their affairs with money and sex causes the scandal.'

'How do you know I'm from the States? With my accent, I could be from Canada.'

She pointed at my sneakers. 'Only a Yank wears trainers outside the gym.'

'Sneakers. I wear sneakers outside the gym and you excoriate me for that? Honor me because I'm an American. If it wasn't for us Yanks, Parisians would be eating knockwurst with sauerkraut and doing the duckwalk.'

'I can say that I appreciate your country.'

'Oh, really? And where are you from?' I asked.

'Surrey. Kingston-up-on-Thames. Just outside of London.'

'London. I should've guessed. And did your parents give you a name?'

'Mary. Catherine Mary Henrietta Potter.' She held out her hand; I shook it.

'Fine, Mary. I am Michael. I wear trainers because they are comfortable to walk in.'

'You should sacrifice comfort for style,' she countered.

'So, how can you both fire barbs at politicians and know so much about fashion?'

'I'm a freelance writer,' she said with a gleam in her eye. 'I write about fashion for newspapers and mags like the Herald Trib, and Elle, and Vogue France, so I have to read the headlines to get a feel for the cultures.'

The waiter came back with a tray of drinks. He and my new friend exchanged pleasantries for a few moments as my beer was placed before me. Mary reached for one of the drinks on the tray and the waiter pulled the tray away quickly. Both of them laughed. The waiter whispered something in Mary's ear and she in turn spoke in his ear. Both of them laughed again. Mary pointed at me and the waiter smiled before he turned to push through the crowd back to the bar.

'I couldn't help but notice,' I said, 'that you were speaking something other than French with the waiter. What language was it you were conversing in?'

'It's Czech. Jiri is from the Czech Republic,' she answered.

'And how do you know Czech?

'A veritable *grande dame* of the Paris fashion district once informed me early in my journalistic career when I was trying to learn French that there is only one true way to learn a foreign language, and that is to hop into bed with a native speaker.'

'Ah, yes. Pillow talk.'

Mary was running her index finger around her glass. 'I speak seven languages fluently,' she said as she placed her lips around her finger.

I got a lump in my throat and swallowed softly, hoping she would not notice.

'So... Do you have a significant other?' she lilted. 'Male or female?'

'The truth is,' I said. 'I am very devoted to my Julia. If not besotted.'

She put her chin in her hand, arched an eyebrow, and with a straight face and a sigh asked me, 'What is truth?'

Chapter V

Olivier's character is hard to describe. Part Sufi Imam, part grunge rocker. And what kind of friend? A good friend. A fine friend. One who would find time to bring me brioches and my favorite *patisseries* for brunch on dreary Sundays when I did not feel like leaving my bed, let alone the apartment. So when he called me to tell me one Saturday evening mid-November that he had a special social engagement for, I had no reason to doubt that it would be a special social engagement to accept. My depression be damned!

With an oversupply of cajoling from both Olivier and Julia, I found myself among some of his work colleagues in Pigalle, a piece of Paris which, as I stated earlier, I often viewed as a landmark to the true dichotomy of a man's own heart – an unstable mixture of sin and salvation. Unfortunately for me, the better side of a man's heart was not to be found that night where we went, since Olivier had surprised me with an invitation to a club (I dare not mention its name) in Pigalle which dabbled in the, ah, flesh trade. *Would Julia approve of this?* I thought and thought while hesitating a few moments at the entrance to the club and blocking a line of surly and growling men behind me.

'Michael, Michael, Michael' said Olivier emphatically. 'You have to learn to deny that little voice inside your head every now and then.'

'Yeah,' I said quietly. 'But that little voice inside my head is pretty loud and can deny me my dinner- and sex. Maybe even lock me out. Or worse.'

'Forget her. Just for an evening.'

I stood before two glass doors, propped open on one side by a crushed soda can and on the other side by a mangy Arab. I pointed to the soda can as Olivier murmured something about this being a classy place and that I should not forget where I am. The mangy Arab told us to keep moving as others behind us wanted to enter. As Olivier grabbed my arm and ushered me in, almost forcibly, my first reaction was one of unsettlement – a feeling that was quickly amplified as I entered the club through its sex paraphernalia shop. The store had a magazine rack and bookshelves dedicated to some of the worst pornography on the planet, as I could quickly ascertain. Pictures of half-naked ladies spread across the walls leading down the hall into the main area of the club. Off to the right was a hallway sign which pointed the way upstairs to the one-Euro video booths. Steely eyed men, impatient and ironically avoiding the eyes of others, were bathed in purple light and seemed to be directionless as they scurried into the club like cockroaches.

Finally, once inside the dance and bar area of the club, I was introduced to Olivier's grim colleagues. One by one I met a slew of men with a common desire to instill life into their very souls, but surely denying they were doing so in the wrong way. And this made for some strange introductions by Olivier. (It is uncanny, but I can say for certain that in a strip-club, like at a spouse's family reunion, people - upon introduction - instantly assume they have become your most intimate of friends. Nauseating in both situations, almost for the same reasons.)

In a few seconds I was seated on an unstable stool at the corner of the bar next to the waitress' entrance to the kitchen – as far away from the dancing girls on stage as I could possibly be, still with an unblocked view of the patrons' dance floor. The smell of greasy food emanating from the kitchen combined with the malodorous chemical cleaner overused on the floors and the bar - if it could be overused - was enough to make me want to wretch in front of God and everybody. Olivier quickly spied my discomfort and ordered me a large mug of *Pelfort Blonde*. The mug was so big it required two hands to lift. Perhaps I had been mistaken; I now foresaw a good start to an evening session with Olivier and company! I took a few quick gulps - enough to calm my nerves and forget what lecture I should be expecting from Julia the next morning when I would confess my actions from this evening.

'Michael, I'd like you to meet someone,' said Olivier as he presented a slender, sexy, slow-moving Negresse with a look that turned men's heads right off their necks. 'Nadya and I met here last summer. I told her about your writing. She does some writing herself.'

'Uh, hello,' I forced out, barely swallowing my beer first.

'Hello,' replied the beautiful Negresse.

'Michael Newman. Nice to meet you,' I said. I waited for her to hold out her hand; it never came.

'Pleasure to meet you. My name is Youna,' she glowed. 'But you can call me *Nadya*.'

'Nice to meet you, Nadya. That is an interesting name. Does it mean anything from your culture?'

'No. Nadya is Slavic. It means *hope*. My father was always so fascinated by Russia. You are a writer? Olivier mentioned to me so.'

'I want to be. I am putting together some of my work for submission. If I ever get the courage to actually submit something.'

'You aren't a writer. Writers don't split infinitives,' she smiled, slowly tilting her head back.

'I did?'

'Yes, you did. You said *to actually submit something.* That is splitting an infinitive and it is incorrect.'

I looked at Olivier. 'She is good.'

'You have *noooooo* idea! Buy her a beer and talk about your writing,' said Olivier. 'Nadya writes in French, and has had some practice writing in English, too. Excuse me, both of you. I have to go talk to Bernard at that table over there about a *soirée* we are planning for Thursday at *Le Violon Dingue*.'

'You know I rarely drink alcohol, Olly. And I see Michael does, too,' Nadya lilted.

'Only to excess. Is that a problem?' I asked.

'You are a teacher?'

'Yes. Yes, I am.'

'How does your school feel about it? Your drinking to excess, I mean?' she asked me.

'What should they care?' I queried lightly.

'Well if you are going to be cruel to yourself, how can God expect you to be compassionate to his creation?'

What could I say? I sheepishly pushed my almost empty mug away from me on the counter.

'Go ahead and drink it. I didn't mean to offend your sensibilities,' she said.

'You didn't,' I said.

'I can see by your face that I truly did.'

'I never could hide my feelings. How do you know English so well?' I asked.

'Don't hide your feelings,' said Nadya. 'Feel them. That is why they are there.'

'I asked you a question.'

'Don't be angry. I just haven't answered you yet. I can tell you are angry.'

'You just told me to feel my feelings and now you tell me not to be angry?' I countered. 'I shouldn't have come here tonight, and I should probably leave now.'

'See what the alcohol is doing to you? It is damaging your sensibilities. It is damaging your sense of self-worth. No wonder you can't publish anything. You are drowning in self-abuse.'

I held my tongue. Oliver came back and pushed a bar-stool next to her. I guess I was angry because he took one look at me and stepped back. As Oliver walked away smiling, Nadya sat casually, as if we were now old friends, and put her small, red-sequin purse on the counter.

'Can I get you *anything* to drink?' I asked as I glanced around the bar looking for the bartender. 'If this place has anything without alcohol?'

'*Richard, eh Richard!*' shouted Nadya. A lumpy man in a silk, chartreuse shirt and overly tight, black pants came out of the kitchen.

Nadya held up two fingers. '*Deux Perrier.* Do you want ice?' she turned to me.

'No. No ice for me,' I replied.

'*Sans glace,*' she said to the barkeep. He pulled two small bottles of sparkling mineral water, uncapped them, and poured them into frosted glasses.

'*Le voila,*' said the barman.

'See? You don't have to drink alcohol here. Or anywhere. To enjoy yourself that is,' Nadya said to me.

'Your English is fantastic for a non-native speaker,' I said. 'How come you speak it so well? You do have an accent, but no grammar mistakes.'

'I started by watching American movies when I was a little girl in Cote d'Ivoire and today I study at The Wall Street Institute down at the Montparnasse Tower,' she replied. 'I

28

have been studying there for over fourteen months. It's where you teach, *non?*'

'Yes. I teach for Wall Street, but I go to the students' locations. I like movies. What movies did you enjoy as a little girl?'

'*Pretty Woman*, with Julia Roberts and Richard Gere. I've seen that one enough times that I can repeat everything Julia Roberts says. And of course there's *American Gigolo*, with Lauren Hutton and Richard Gere,' she said.

'I think I see a trend. Why the focus on prostitution?' I asked.

'Olivier did not tell you much about me, I think,' she smiled. 'It's not just a focus; it's how I live.'

'You are a prostitute?' I said choking on my mineral water.

'It's how I eat, and pay for my English and writing lessons. Let's not make an issue of it, shall we?' she hinted at her disdain.

'I just thought you were interested in me and my writing,' I smirked.

'Sorry to disappoint you. Be careful or you may offend my sensibilities.'

'I often do that to women,' I said.

'That is unfortunate. For you.'

'I know,' I opined. 'I should never be allowed to talk to women, ever.'

'How does your wife take you?' she asked.

I stumbled with my drink in hand, nearly dropping it on the floor.

'Oh so sensitive are we?' she asked.

'About a few things that could lead to more depression, yes,' I stated.

She patted my hand softly.

I changed subjects. 'Let's talk about writing, shall we?'

'Fine with me, Michael. What do you most write about?' she asked.

'People. And their lives. Not altogether anything personal, but their lives as relating to my own. Just mini-sketches, mostly.'

'I like to write about humor. Can you tell me anything humorous about people and their lives?'

'Well,' I offered. 'I'm not sure life is funny, but people say funny things. Recently I heard one French student say in an open forum at the Sorbonne that in Mid-East policy there needs to be more *copulation* between U.S. and European governments.'

'What is copulation?'

'Umm, sex.'

'Hah!' Nadya threw her head back.

'More sex is a good idea,' I continued. 'But maybe not between governments.'

'That's the kind of situation I want to read about.'

'The unplanned inanities in life.'

'Ah, but better,' she smiled. 'to live and to see humor in life. Tell me more.'

'Well…' I began. 'One teacher asked her student if her hair color was natural. *No*, the student answered. *My hair is dead.*'

'Hah!' Nadya threw her head back again. 'Her hair is dead! That's better than, what's the word you just used?'

'Copulation.'

'That's something funny to build upon in your writing.'

'Actually, I don't always build on humorous lines, though that helps. I like to expound on the philosophical pinges that-'

'Pinges?' she asked. 'I've never heard this word. What is a pinge?'

'It's a word I made up. Pinge sort of means anecdote, but it is more cognitive than that, like something you know to be true but can't put into words easily.'

'And that's what you write about?' she asked me. 'About cognitive pinges, philosophy, and all that can't be put into words easily?'

'Yes.'

'We have little in common then.' She took a drink of her mineral water and looked away. 'But why this word pinge?'

'It's short for impinge, as in impinge upon someone,' I answered. 'The cognitive pinges affect people, even push them and egg them on to do something uncommon, but they cannot be described easily. Sometimes thinking is just like that; you do something but can't explain why. It juts feels right.'

'I believe it is called emotion.'

'It's more than emotion. It is thinking that can't be defined. Clear, rational cognition that drives action which none can explain!' I elaborated. 'Like when a driver in an accident says he hit the tree which wasn't there before. Has this never happened to you?'

'You've had too much beer tonight, Michael,' her eyebrow raised. 'But entertain me; give me a better example.'

'It's like when you say goodbye to someone and then run into them around the block. That indescribable cognition – it isn't emotion - of not knowing what to say. It's a pinge.'

'Do you get this problem often?'

'Not quite, but I-'

'Kiss me. Now.' She leaned forward and put her hand on my knee.

'Wha-?' I said as Nadya planted a wet one on my cheek.

Olivier came stumbling up with a tall, muscular man in a tight black t-shirt. A much taller, very thin man with oval eyeglasses and a fuchsia shirt unbuttoned to the navel followed. The three of them stopped right between Nadya and me and almost knocked us both into the bar.

'This is Tim. He's from Sweden. Behind him is P.G.; he's a Yank, like you.'

'I like your chest P.G.,' said Nadya sexily as she pushed Olivier aside and reached into the thin man's open shirt. 'Too bad it has no hair on it.'

'Hey, girl, grass doesn't grow on a playgound!' the thin man crowed at such a decibel I could barely stand to hear it.

'You two know each other?' asked Olivier incredulously.

'Yes, we know each other,' Nadya answered. 'But don't worry about him.' She held up a finger and a thumb, 'P.G. has small one.'

'Hey, baby, it's not the angle of the dangle,' P.G. thrusted his pelvis. 'It's the size of the rise.'

'How unattractive,' Olivier said. 'I guess that I have no need to explain to you P.G.'s proclivities then.'

'Oh, I know P.G.,' said Nadya. 'When I first met him *mono a mono* with his pants down, I started to laugh. Then he tells me that it's not the size of the boat, but the motion in the ocean.'

'That's right, baby,' said P.G. thrusting his pelvis again.

'Has Nadya dazzled you with her insight into humanity?' Olivier asked looking at me.

'She did inform me that she has a lot of, um, experience with people, especially men. But really we were speaking mostly of *my* writing,' I replied.

'Did she tell you that her father was a diplomat and that he went to Cambridge? Did she tell you she studied in the American school in Abidjan? And that she was kicked out of the eleventh grade for having sex with her English professor?' he continued unabated, rather loudly, I felt.

Nadya put her hands on her hips. Tim, the muscular Swede, gave us a bored look and walked away. Olivier just waved a hand.

'No, she hadn't told me that. Yet,' I said.

'Well, you have much to learn about her,' said Olivier. 'And she will tell you much, no doubt, because she knows so much. She has been around the world in the care of diplomats like her father, as she will tell you, I'm sure. She has seen exotic countries, met inspiring people, and soaked up different cultures like water on dry earth. She is comfortable in any conversation, whether cosmopolitan or provincial in nature. An experienced professional escort in all hedonism has to offer. She rivals your Julia in-'

Nadya put a hand to her mouth and coughed.

'Oh, I *am* sorry. Did I say something wrong?'

P.G. interrupted, 'See that old brunette woman in the corner? The one with the goiter? She's a true blue Dutchie. I just went up to her and asked her if she'd screw me for a hundred Euro. She said no. I then asked her if she'd screw me for a thousand Euro. She said no again. I then opened my wallet and asked her if she'd screw me for ten thousand Euro. She thought a moment, smiled, and said yes. So I pulled a fifty Euro note out and grabbed her arm and said let's go. So she goes, *What's with the fifty Euro? What kind of lady do you think I am?* So I says, *Well, we have already established that, now lets negotiate a price.*'

'Olly, maybe you and P.G. should go dance. With each other,' said Nadya.

'Sure. We will leave you two to discuss your, uh, writings, yes?' said Olivier chuckling.

Olivier reach for P.G. by his thin arm and led him away while whispering into his ear. Both of them laughed without turning around. Nadya turned to me and started giggling.

'I am sorry, Nadya,' I spoke. 'But I don't want to stay out late and I am feeling a little depressed inside this place. I have been feeling depressed a lot lately.'

'You are not enjoying my company. I am hurt,' she blinked.

'I am enjoying your company. It is just that I am not enjoying this place. Maybe we could meet some afternoon when I am not teaching and discuss our writings.'

'Pinges,' she said smiling. 'I've learned something here tonight with you.'

'Yes. Pinges.'

'Will you finish your Perrier with me before you leave me here all alone with these brutes?' she asked shyly. 'Please?'

'A toast then to the porno-flesh palaces of gay Paree,' I offered.

'Yes,' Nadya answered. 'You meet the most interesting people in them.'

Chapter VI

Nadya got me thinking about philosophy and literature after that bizarre meeting; I am not sure why. I like literature and, for the most part, I understand it. And I like philosophy, even though most often I get lost in it. Sometimes it's difficult for me to make a definite distinction between the two, because when I discuss one I end up using the other for reference. But my fractured knowledge of both influence my making of many decisions, especially if I can't find a real person with whom to discuss my issues. And in Paris my only issues were depression and… alcohol.

When I started to ruminate in Paris about possibly giving up alcohol, I turned to some familiar sources, which were not necessarily directly on top of the issue, but contained enough adequate reasoning to influence my decision. I asked people, if they were around. I checked the Bible. I read literature. Not necessarily in that order, or with any order at all, but always in a veritable search of the answer to my question: *should I drink?*

On a loose philosophical bent, I started with the basics. If I understand the writings of the German philosopher, Hegel, sufficiently, society is spiraling positively upward and upward, advancing consistently (by medical developments and social improvements, for example) with a few, inevitable, negative dips (such as world wars, global warming, and disco dancing). And despite the few, unavoidable nicks and mars, the individual life's spiral progression toward a holistic betterness will always, Hegel believed, move us upward collectively towards a better society.

So I wondered, specifically after Nadya's lambasting of my love for alcohol, where actually does man's invention of alcohol find place on the long-term spiral of civilization: as an upward turn on the spiral or a downward dip?

A friend sent me an email on the topic. 'Alcohol is that magic invention' says my friend Eric, 'that turns a weekday into Saturday night, and turns Saturday night into New Year's Eve.' Not much help, was he.

I heard my cousin the Catholic priest once give a homily that an action can be determined to be sinful from analyzing the end result of the experience. (Whether this is true for pre-marital sex: the jury is still out. Okay, I give, this is not true. But I did have a definitive problem saying no to my rather ebullient hormones in my early adulthood.) As for my after-experiences of drinking alcohol to excess, I would usually wake up around three in the afternoon, feeling like I slept with a stinky wool stocking in my mouth, only to look in the scratched mirror and see Edvard Munch's *The Scream* staring back. Then, while shaking my head, I would listen to the morning's taped phone messages from my friends extolling my previous night's beery machinations of kissing girls who look like Schnauzers and urinating on parked BMWs. After all this pleasantry, if I am most determined to try to put something organic in my stomach, I am really only moments away of nothing less fun than staring at a pool of my own gastic juices as I pray to the porcelain goddess, swearing to God and His Heaven above that I will never, ever – cross my heart and hope to die – drink alcohol again. (Of course this feeling only lasts for a day and then I am out looking for another good spirits-filled time. The end result was horrific, that was sure, but as we all know, it doesn't last.)

Still, with my cousin the priest commenting and my listening not-so-intently, I thought there must surely be something the other CIA (Catholic Irish Alcoholics) in my family would conjecture about the issue. But when it comes to alcohol and religion, I have no unbiased family members because one is so much a part of the other. If I wanted a religious perspective, I needed to go to *the* source.

Interestingly, the Bible has something to say about the end result of drinking, this very sequence of events I mentioned above. I unabashedly quote Proverbs 23: 29-35.

Who has woe? Who has sorrow? Who has strife? Who has complaints? Who has needless bruises? Who has bloodshot eyes? Those who linger over wine, who go to sample bowls of mixed wine. Do not gaze at wine when it is red, when it sparkles in the cup, when it goes down smoothly! In the end it bites like a snake and poisons like a viper. Your eyes will see strange sights and your mind imagine confusing things. You will be like one sleeping on the high seas, lying on top of the rigging. 'They hit me,' you will say, 'but I am not hurt! They beat me, but I don't feel it! When will I wake up so I can find another drink?'

When will I wake up so I can find another drink. Some would say that this point is baseless, but the writer – the great King Solomon - concludes that the problem has no end, that it is cyclical, and that it is obviously a dip on an individual's spiral. So much for the Bible's take on the issue. I wonder what Hegel would say about Solomon's spiral and his demise.

But this Bible thing, as I have mentioned before, interests me deeply. I don't think the Bible has it anywhere definitive that God will smite me for imbibing to excess the sacramental fruit of the vine (but I do believe a piece of my soul dies when I do). The Bible leaves me hanging again.

I tried discussing this scriptural matter in a holier-than-none vein, first with Julia, who as usual, with restraint and patience, told me to put my Bible away and get real, and second with Nadya, who suggested I take up the issue with the real person from whom I needed to get permission to stop drinking from: my partner during the fun side of alcoholism, Olivier.

I brought my Bible to my next social outing (read: drinking session) with Olivier on the steps of *Sacre Coeur* after having pondered to mental exhaustion my wavering decision to quit drinking, ready to quote scripture should he want to see any holy leans as proof to support an otherwise impractical choice. As I climbed the narrow, crowded steps up *Montmartre* and saw the crowd of North Africans dancing next to Olivier and his friends, who were enjoying their music and drinking warmed over bottles of beer, I lost my footing, stumbled and dropped my Bible on a wrinkly, old woman, much as I guess Moses stumbled down Mount Sinai and dropped the stone tablets of the Ten Commandments when he saw his people dancing around the golden calf. The old woman looked at the cover of the great book, flipped through a few pages, shook her head, and solemnly handed it back to me without looking me in the eye. With this bad omen and the fact, I would soon learn, that Olivier brought a bottle of Madeira, his favorite drink and one that is hard for me to turn away, maybe this wasn't the time to bring up the issue of getting on the wagon. When I was finally standing next to him on the steps, I chose to be silent in this cacaphony around me, and I looked off into the distance toward the *Centre George Pompidou*. Olivier grabbed my arm, pulled me a few steps, and sat me down on the grassy slope next to the stone steps. A droopy mastiff lying lazily next to us barely raised his head to greet us; the dog's owner eyed us curiously.

'Whassup, Newman?' he asked. 'You look like you don't want to be here. It's one of the best times of the year, now, the *faux printemps* now – the false spring. We is lucky to have a such warm day so early in the new year, so youz better enjoy it whilst it lasts. Here, let's 'ave a drink.' He held forth the bottle of Madeira.

I looked at my shoes. 'I'm thinking of giving up alcohol, *mon ami*,' I told Olivier. 'However hypocritical that sounds as I ponder enjoying that luscious bottle of Madeira in your hand.'

'Giving up alcohol? What the hell? What the hell for?' he asked. 'Is it Julia? It's Julia, isn't it? She has made the hammer to fall.'

'No, it isn't my Julia. Really, it's... my health,' I answered flatly. 'My mental health.'

'Your mental health. *Christo*. You can't give up alcohol, *mon ami*. I'll die.'

'You can't die. Where will they entomb your brain safely? Look, it even says on the bottle that alcohol is bad for one's health,' I offered. 'Look at it.'

'It says on this bottle that pregnant women shouldn't drink it. But if it weren't for alcohol, there would be no pregnant women,' he countered.

'How humorous. You never quit, do you?' I asked rhetorically.

'Neither do you. This bottle of Madeira enhances life, Michael; who then cares if it shortens it?' Olivier asked. 'Health is a secondary concern to a Parisian when compared to enjoying each day as best as possible. Health is so very, very unimportant. Don't worry about health in life – life's too short. Focus on what makes you come alive. Look around you! The world is best with people who are ALIVE! For us and those around us now - part of this experience- it's the alcohol, just one of the many, delicious material gifts of God which make us come alive.'

The mastiff stood up and shook himself. He and the owner walked down the grassy hill.

I took a breath and relaxed. 'Health may be a trifle to a Parisian, I accept. But even trifles are important,' I countered gracefully.

'Says who?'

'Rascalnikov.'

'Who the hell's Rascal Nickel? As if I care about your *faux philosophe* friends.'

'Rascalnikov. He's not one of my friends; he's Dostoyevsky's hero character in *Crime and Punishment*. In the opening pages, Rascalnikov has a tussle with his landlady and says, I quote, trifles are important.'

'Dostoyevsky means trifles about *people* between people are important because a human life is so short, like smoke,' Olivier said as he poured some of the Madeira into a rocks glass. 'I am sure that is what he means. Relating to people is important, and inevitable in all polite societies, unless I guess you're a hermit. Relationships are the only thing you can have which is valuable in a human life. That is what he means; I am sure of it.'

'Maybe so,' I forced out weakly.

'Dostoyevsky was a gifted writer, dammit, but wasn't Dostoyevsky a heavy drinker?'

'Yes, he was a drunken sot.'

'If you want to write, then like all writers great and small, you *will* have your affairs, *mon ami*. Affairs for men always start with alcohol, then they include women, and then when the money is all gone, the fickle, gold-digging women leave, and it is back to alcohol again.'

Yes, he was right: I took my desire to be a writer seriously. And it is well known that all writers drink. But it is not known that all writers drink, I believe, because writing is hell. I stammered, and thought and thought while still not looking him in the eye. I could summon no reasoning to counter him. Olivier put his hand on my shoulder.

'Very well. Do what you want, Baptist. This conversation is sobering me up,' Olivier complained. 'If you choose to continue it, I will choose to leave you to your own boringness and I will go back to my own fun with my bottle. I took a nap this afternoon with a bottle of vodka as a pillow.'

I looked at Olivier and pinched my lip. His eyes were already bloodshot. He just shrugged his shoulders and smiled. What could I do? I was there and there was no reason to want to ruin Olivier's evening, and what a beautiful evening it was turning out to be up there in front of the *Sacre Cœur*. For Christ's sake, Olivier had shown up this time at *Montmartre* for me. *Just for me!* I thought. *Dammit, he is a good friend. The best.*

Moving quickly, I pulled a rocks glass from my backpack and let Olivier pour me a short drink of the Madeira. I changed the subject to the box scores of the spring European rugby games.

'That's the Michael I know well,' he hissed, eyes squinting.

Trifles about people are important, I would repeat to myself often in Paris. And my relationship with Olivier was an important trifle. Even with the alcohol.

Chapter VII

Nadya called me on a Saturday morning close to Christmas. Would I like to go shopping with her for presents for her nieces? 'Of course!' I said. 'I love to shop with other people's money.'

We met at *Chatelet* underneath the statue and walked up *Boulvard Sebastopol* towards *Les Halles*, turning left on *Rambuteau*, then heading to the escalators down to the expansive underground shopping center. For being so close to Christmas, the usual bumbling crowd was a little light. Nadya seemed a little put off when I asked her how her week went, and I said I was just trying to be friendly. For some odd reason, she told me that it was none of my business.

We walked what seemed like miles around the twists and turns of the great undergound mall, and only backtracked when we got to the public pool, which wreaked of chlorine.

'Michael, you look a little down. Is something wrong?'

'My shipment of deodorant hasn't come in yet from the States.'

'Why don't you buy some here,' she asked.

'Because I am allergic to it, unfortunately.'

'So what are you going to do?'

'Smell like the French.'

'Let's go in this clothing store, Michael. It looks like there might be something to fit me.'

'I thought we were shopping for your nieces?'

Suddenly, she let out a squeal that I would not want to hear twice in my life.

Nadya pulled a nice calico dress out, and laid it against her body. I shook my head. A few minutes later, she took out another dress, this one mauve and crimson. I shook my head again. I was still feeling hurt that she had slighted me twice already that day, and no apologies were forthcoming.

As can be expected in Paris, the saleswoman was in a snippy mood, and unwilling to be bothered to answer questions for Nadya about the two dresses. Maybe it was racism; maybe the saleswoman was having the usual bad day at work in Paris. I, of course, knew what that was like. We left the shop disappointed.

'Michael, I am hungry. Let's go eat.'

'The *James Joyce* has a good meal cheap. And can we get a bottle of wine? I am feeling parched.'

'Let's go!'

The *James Joyce* is a fun and funky Irish bar on the Northern edge of *Les Halles*, just around the corner from the Catholic basilica, *Saint Eustache*- how appropriate. We bounced around on the cobblestone steps, like we were playing as children, for a few minutes. Then we stepped into the *Joyce*. Empty, it was.

The floor was sticky, and the air wreaked of stale beer, as is to be expected in any hole run by British commoners, such as the Joyce was. Seating ourself at the zinc bar, the bartender was busy watching a rugby game on an old black and white television situated above the various cheap alcohols on the wall. I am not sure if he had not noticed us walk in or he was just too busy with his game to care, but this set off Nadya.

'Excuse me!' Nadya yelled.

The barkeep kept to the game.

'If you have an Irish accent, I will take my clothes off for you!'

'Whassat you say, bird?' the barkeep turned around.

'I said I want to order some lunch. And I am not one of your birds!'

'Kitchen's closed,' he said as he turned back to his game. 'We had a grease fire last night. I can get you a drink.'

'Never mind, poof' said Nadya. 'We are hungry. Let's split, Michael.'

On our way out, I asked the guy mopping the floor who won the rugby game between the Americans and the South African Springboks.

'America got stuffed, as usual. Looks like you are gonna get stuffed later, bloke,' the mate said with a wink.

Nadya pulled me outside impatiently.

'Do you think that bartender was camp, Michael?'

'A poof? Unsure.'

'Who can resist this body?' she said gayly as she ran her hands over her tight clothing. 'I'll bet he was camp.'

'I really have no idea. Actually, I think he is asexual. He spores.'

'Michael, do you think I am sexy?'

'Sexy? In what way?'

Nadya's mien wilted.

We decided to walk north of *Les Halles* to find a small Arab place serving *sandwich grecs*. We came across one I had never seen, let alone been to, before, and wouldn't you know it, there was an open *Nicholas* wine store a half block away. *Nicholas* is generally more expensive for wines, but still, this was good news!

'Sweets, go on into the Arab's, and I will pick us up some wine for the meal.'

'Won't the Arabs say no to letting us bring in the alcohol?' she asked.

'No. It's hypocritical, but they want our money too much.'

With that we separated for a few moments, Nadya going inside the Arab's, and me walking to the open *Nicholas*. As soon as I walked in and opened my mouth and spoke a few words in French, the petite middle-aged man working behind the counter asked me if I were American.

'*So what if I am?*

'*We have a nice chardonnay for you.*'

'*Chardonnay? Be real! I'm not that American. I want red. Looking for a deal on a merlot. What can you show me, good sir?*'

'*I have a 98 Paulliac bordeax on sale. Only 36 euro.*'

'*I am looking for something a bit more… pedestrian,*' I said without shame. '*What is the cheapest red you have?*'

'*Chateau Charmant. Still a tete de cuvee. Eleven euro.*'

I sighed. Eleven euro was better than an hour's wages for me, but it was a nice Saturday for Nadya and me, and I decided to splurge a little. '*I'll take two, please.*' I handed over my *carte bleu* and the store employee rang up the two bottles. I turned to leave, and he went to the backroom, neither of us saying 'goodbye' or 'thanks' now that the deal was consummated. Such is life in gay *Paree*.

When I went back to the Arab store, Nadya was seated at the counter looking out into the Paris drizzle. Her hands were folded on the dirty counter, and she had a look of concern on her face.

'Look, sweets. Two bottles. One and a half for me, and, well, the rest for you,' I said with a smile.

'Great, Michael.'

Food was ordered, and, seeing that we were the only patrons in this dive, quickly served.

'The french fries are soggy,' Nadya pointed out depressedly.

'Well, I have my bottle of *Charmant*. Can we ask for a knife to open it?'

Nadya went up to the service counter and asked for a knife and two glasses. The mangy Arab wiped a dull knife on a clean napkin and held it up for her. A moment later he produced two glasses.

'Who needs a corkscrew?' I asked rhetorically. I took the knife in my right hand and the bottle of red wine in my left. I cut the foil and pulled it off in one twist. *That's good luck*, I thought.

I turned the bottle in my hand a few times to look for a good position. With the knife, I stroked the bottle from the base of the neck up to just below the lip. Each stroke was sound and deliberate, and my hand moved in a practiced, fluid motion. Each time the knife struck below the lip with the sound of a small glass breaking. Again and again I stroked the bottle with the knife, never failing to hit the lip in exactly the same place. After fourteen or fifteen strokes, the clinking sound changed. I had managed to break the bottle around the lip. The glass did not shatter because the cork protected it. The break was circular around the lip.

Nadya smiled at the sound of the cracking lip. 'You do that so well,' she said.

I grabbed a napkin and placed it around the top of the bottle. I pulled on the lip and the piece of glass slid off the cork easily. *Good*, I thought. *The cork is well moistened so it will come off easily as well.* I put the cork in my teeth and pulled, being careful not to cut my mouth. The cork popped out with a hollow sound. *Never fails*, I said. *Who needs a corkscrew?* I wiped the top of the bottle with the napkin and inspected for bits of glass. I then poured a little of the wine into an empty glass. Precious few small pieces of cork floated in the ruby red wine – *Nicholas* sells the best bottles in all of Paris. I swished the glass, looking at the oily draw along the sides of the glass. 'It's crying,' I pointed out to Nadya. Smiling, I raised the glass for a smell.

'Mmmm,' I said, passing the glass to Nadya for a quick sniff.

I tasted the wine, spit it out into an empty soda can, and dumped the rest of the glass into the same soda can to remove the cork bits. Nadya handed me a ruffled napkin to wipe the glass clean. I then filled the two glasses halfway and sat down on the circular stool. We quickly finished off one glass each, and then another, before we started eating the sandwiches. Nadya only took a few small bites.

'Nadya, you look concerned. Something a little more wine can help?'

She looked at me. 'I've been thinking all day since we met. How did he do it?'

'How did who do what? Drink your wine – it will help your disposition.'

'Your father. How did he do it?'

'Gads. Bottle of sleeping pills. You gonna eat and drink or depress me on this drizzly day?'

'Does it still affect you?'

'I scream in my sleep. Have done it for years. Mother sent me to a psychiatrist as a child, but to no avail.'

'Then why did Jesus have to die?'

'What does one have to do with the other?' I asked as I started to open the other bottle of red.

'Look what He did to you.'

'My father?'

'No, Jesus. He just...He just put so much pain in you. Into your life.'

'Kurt Vonnegut wrote a fantastic novel – can't recall the title right now – in which at one point the main character talks about a machine used by automakers to bend and stress cars to find their breaking point. He likens God's making this world with all its pain thus for humans to that machine.'

'Is that how you see the world?'

'No. I rather see the world as a giant sink, in which Jesus is washing us clean on the inside. In preparation for heaven, I mean.'

'I need to talk to a priest. I have put off my questions for far too long.'

'Now?'

'As soon as you are ready.'

'Let's finish here first.'

Nadya only picked at her food, and stopped my pouring for her at the next glass of wine. I continued to drink, but left the greasy food which was starting to get cold. I could tell Nadya was anxious to go find a priest – for whatever reason she wasn't willing to explain to me- and the alcohol wasn't helping. Still, I did not want to chug the rest of the wine. When both bottles were empty, we left the Arab store in search of a priest.

'We can go back to *Saint Eustache* church?' I pitched.

'No. I know another church,' said Nadya. '*Saint Germain L'Auxerrois*. It is near the Louvre. I heard Valerie Giscard D'Estang goes there.'

'Near the Louvre? That's at least ten long blocks away!'

'We are going,' she said grabbing my hand and pulling me fast.

Nothing like breaking into a fast walk after sucking down a bottle and a half of wine and some greasy food. By the time we got to the church, I was out of breath and ready to wretch right there on the sidewalk.

Nadya thankfully slowed down the last few steps as we reached *Saint Germain L'Auxerrois* church and started to look for an open entrance. A very thin man with taught skin over hollow cheeks was pushing a green, custodian wash-bin through the main church entrance, and Nadya went ahead and introduced herself to him.

'Hello. We'd like to talk to a priest please. Can you tell us how we might find one here?'

'What do you want with the old priest?' asked the gaunt custodian with a cracking voice. *'A condom?'*

'No thank you,' said Nadya. *'We just want to ask him a few questions about Jesus.'*

'Why do you want to question him about Jesus? What do you care what he thinks? He isn't going to tell you your fornication is okay.'

'WE ARE NOT FORNICATING!' Nadya yelled. *'Will you please summon the priest for us or at least tell us which entrance to knock on?'*

'Isn't she a little young for you, my good man?' the custodian turned to me with a wink.

'Don't be so snooty. You are as young as the woman you feel,' I said in return.

'Oh! You both are making me crazy!' said Nadya. *'I will look for the priest myself. This is important for me. Are you with me, Michael, or not? I want to know now!'*

'Look. Here comes Father Cordier now. Don't tell him you are sleeping with her, or he will get upset.'

'Gustav, is everything okay?' the jowly priest asked in a smooth baritone vox.

'Yes, everything is fine, Father. These young people are wanting to ask you a few questions about Jesus. I was just telling them how delighted you would be to help them.'

'Oh, they do. Very well. How pleasant for me to have company this day. Would you young people care to follow me into the vestibule and out of the cold? Thank you, Gustav.'

'Father, I think they have been tipping the bottle some.' He held a finger and thumb to his mouth.

'*That is quite alright. Carry on, Gustav. You are doing a fine job, yes a fine job here. Come with me, my dear children,*' he reached out a wrinkly and spotted hand.

We walked through the expansive wood and wrought-iron doors into *St. Germain* church.

'*You will have to excuse Gustav if he was rude to you,*' said the aged priest. '*He hasn't been feeling well lately.*'

'*Why is he so thin?*' asked Nadya.

'*Yes, he is thin and very, very frail. The poor Romanian has AIDS.*'

The priest murmured an incomprehensible prayer and bowed as we passed the altar and went towards his study to the left of the sanctuary. Once seated in nice, red velvet upholstered chairs, I relaxed. *Quite the tranquilizer, a church and an old priest can be*, I thought. Nadya was still very emotional.

'*Now, my dear children. What are your questions?*'

'*Well, Father-*' I started to speak.

'*Why did Jesus have to die?*' asked Nadya, almost despondent.

'*A very good question! It is no secret: Jesus died for your sins. Yours and mine. That is why He died, because He loves you more than you can understand. And the only saving grace was giving Himself up for us all on the cross.*'

'*But why?*' asked Nadya. '*Why was He crucified? He gave to the poor. He served the needy. He listened to others and prayed for them. And He spoke of such marvelous things! I just don't understand why He was whipped and killed.*'

'*You have a good understanding of the events of His short life, my dear. But if you read the Holy Passages again, you will see that Jesus was tortured and crucified because He said that He was God. And to the Jewish people of His time, that was blasphemy.*'

'*I know a street-walker back in D.C. who thinks he is god, too, but nobody is crucifying him. They just force him to take a lot of medications,*' I said.

'*Michael, be serious!*' demanded Nadya. '*This is important for me.*'

'*Young man, how much have you had to drink today?*' asked the priest.

'*Only an excessive amount.*'

'*And yes, a funny young man at that. Jesus drank wine, but He doesn't approve of your flagrant drunkenness. You should be more careful with your life. Or it may be a short one. Look at how sickly you are feeling now, and trust that feeling.*'

'*What can you tell me about heaven, Father?*' asked Nadya.

The priest turned back towards Nadya. '*Ah, a very good question! Not much is known about heaven, my dear daughter. The Bible speaks of roads of gold and pearly gates, but that is it. Think of yourself here on earth like a baby in a mother's womb. He cannot know what the world will be like until he is born; all one can know is faint sounds and gurgles from outside the womb. That is how you are now, waiting to be born to a new and everlasting life.*'

'*Father, what do you think of the rapid growth of the Muslim population in France?*' I redirected.

'*For which do you choose, son, heaven or hell?*' the priest said with a frown.

'*You want me to choose between heaven or hell? I break a sweat in front of a jukebox.*'

'*Do you know why the Muslim religion is the fastest growing religion in France and the world?*' he asked me.

'*No. No. I guess I don't. Why?*'

His eyes narrowed. '*Because a Muslim man is willing to die for his beliefs. Hardly a Christian man today is willing to do that. Many Muslim men will willingly give up their sons and even their daughters in Jihad.*'

'*So what does that mean for me? I am a Catholic like you.*'

'*Sic vi pacem, paro bellum.*'

'*Oh, yes, Latin. Yes, fine. I took four years of Latin at Williston. Can you repeat that?*'

'*Sic vi pacem, paro bellum. It means, if you want peace, prepare for war.*'

'*I see. There is a war between Christians and Muslims?*'

'*Yes, it is starting. And it will only become more severe over time, I am afraid.*'

'*Yes, well, I know I am on the right side at least,*' I said proudly.

'*The land underneath the U.S. Embassy here in Paris, who owns the land?*'

'*Um, France? I would think that-*'

'*No, the U.S. owns the land underneath the U.S. Embassy. And it is the same with every sovereign embassy in the world. It's just as Jesus owns you- an Ambassador for Christ, you are! So your body containing Christ's Spirit is like an embassy for Jesus' Kingdom here deep within Satan's territory. Wherever Jesus goes with you, there is His Kingdom. Show it by your good works in the world, instead of drinking so much and making ignorant cracks.*'

'*I can only imagine why you are telling me all this. It's because you can tell I haven't taken Communion in a while, right? Yes, Father, I am trying my best to be an Ambassador for Christ, but-*'

'*Then don't drink so much, I tell you. At least don't drink so early in the day. If you drink early in the day, it means you have a problem with alcohol.*'

'*I used to have a problem with alcohol. Now I can afford it.*'

'*Do you have any further questions which I can help you with?*' asked the righteous man.

'*Can you comment on the Catholic clergy sex-abuse scandal?*'

The priest's face fell. '*The closer a man gets to God, the closer he fights with Satan.*' He turned to look with concern at Nadya. '*Why are you crying, young lady?*'

'*Because she, too, had a little too much of the Blood of Christ at lunch today, Father,*' I said.

'*No! It is because no one will help me with my questions!*' exclaimed Nadya, as she sobbed on.

'*I am trying to help you, my darling,*' said the priest. '*What is it in your heart you wish to discuss?*'

'*I already told you. Why did Jesus have to die? I mean, why? His Father sent Him to earth to die? It just doesn't make sense.*'

'*Jesus had to die for your sins. That is called the Atonement.*'

'*But why? I don't understand why that had to happen.*'

'*For the forgiveness of your sins.*'

'*You're still not answering me. Why did he have to die? Why couldn't He just say a prayer and that be it? He had to be tortured and crucified? Was that a part of the plan the Father made? Then the Father could have changed the Law, right? If He is Omnipotent, then He could have changed the Law. I don't understand at all,*' Nadya cried on.

The priest looked at me, both of us apoplectic. Unfortunately, my buzz was starting to wear off, and I did not want to end the afternoon sober. I surely needed more wine.

'*Sweets, I think we need to go for a walk. The sun is coming out. Let's go for a walk and get a crepe au chocolat. Does that sound good?*' I offered.

'*Yes. Fine, let's go. Sorry to have bothered you, Father.*'

'*It's quite alright. No problem at all, actually. I appreciate your wonder and curiosity at the Divinity of Christ. Keep your candles burning. You are the light of the world. Do you have any further questions I can help you with, my dear children?*'

'*Just one more, Father. The word Noel,*' I said.

'*Yes, what about it?*'

'*The word El means God in Hebrew. So are we saying no God, or no to God, when we say No...El?*'

With that, the old priest frowned and rubbed his brow with his hand. He labored slowly to lift himself out of the velvet-rimmed chair, rubbing his knee as he stood. Nadya and I stood up obligingly. The priest walked straight at me with a limp I had not noticed earlier. We all shook hands gently, the upright vicar smiled good-naturedly, and he turned slowly to lead us out of his study.

Chapter VIII

On a warm Saturday in early February, late morning, two weeks after I told Olivier I was giving up alcohol, I had a surprising freshness in my spirit and had the soulful drive to venture out into Paris humanity on my own after a morning cup of apple-mint tea. (Surprising, I say, because I had called in sick the last three days from my teaching job because I couldn't drag my deeply-depressed self out of bed. Julia had had enough of my insipid lethargy and left me for her job in Montparnasse.) And just as I was leaving for this venture out alone with my cap and sunglasses and a Coca-Cola Light, Nadya called me to say that she and Charlie were meeting that afternoon and would I like finally to meet with him, too? I accepted the fine invitation, grabbed my couriour's bag and *carte orange* and headed toward the metro, stopping only to pick up a brioche to munch on the train. I was hungry for sweet pastry and plentiful sunshine: a good sign. While on the train I managed to scratch a few words on my yellow legal pad to show Nadya what I had been thinking about since I last talked to her. I certainly couldn't show up to meet her with no new writing to impress her with, could I?

Nadya and I met at the fountain at St. Michel and walked along the south side of the Seine river toward Notre Dame to meet Charlie. She hadn't much to say to me and really only commented glibly on the cool Paris drizzle that had rolled in to put an end to the nice warm morning. I could tell she was preoccupied with our meeting Charlie, and her personal distance to me combined with the cacaphonic traffic squelched any chance for conversation. We headed off to meet Charlie in the direction of the *quai d'Orsay*.

Charlie was standing outside of Shakespeare and Company Books rummaging through the stacks and crates of the crassly-treated, used literature when Nadya first spotted him. George Whitman, Shakespeare and Company's proprietor, was leaning against the front door in the drizzle while looking across the fast-moving Seine towards Notre Dame.

Nadya quickened her pace when she saw Charlie in the light rain. For a slow mannered Negresse, she could really hustle when she felt the need. 'Just look at him,' she said as we neared. 'Isn't he beautiful?' I just looked at her.

'Hello, darling Charlie,' she said, coming up to him and kissing him on both cheeks.

'Whill,' Charlie said slightly taken aback, like he was addressing a child softly. 'How good to see you on this perfect day in our paradise.'

'Yes,' she answered, kissing him on both cheeks again. 'It is another fine day in our paradise. How have you been?'

'Or as the French say *Comment garbanzo?*' he chuckled.

'What?' Nadya looked confused.

David looked at me and winked. 'How you *bean?*'

I had to laugh at this. Charlie kept one eye fixed on me, or so I felt.

'You must introduce me to your friend,' said Charlie, still looking at me, as he raised a wrinkled hand in my direction.

'Charlie, this is my newfound Paris friend, Michael,' said Nadya. Charlie held out his bony hand for me to shake. And shake we did, for even in his advanced years his grip was startlingly tight.

'Michael, this is my teacher and confidant, Charlie,' Nadya introduced. 'He's a minor celebrity in the leather jacket and cigarette crowd attending the *Beaux Arts* School. I know him from his creative discussions on modern existentialism and religion at the *Café de Flore*.'

'A minor celebrity? I relish your compliment, Whill,' Charlie said. 'But even at my eighty-third year of life, my artwork still has a lot of evolving to do. That's my focus now: the evolution of my artwork.'

'Did he call you *Will*?' I questioned.

'Charlie calls me Whill,' answered Nadya. 'It's a long story.'

'Oh,' I said, waiting for her to go on. (She didn't.)

Nadya pointed a mocha hand at me. 'Michael is the gifted writer who told me about the student at the Sorbonne forum saying *copulation* between governments, instead of cooperation.'

'Yes, I do remember you mentioning that to me,' Charlie said as he lit up a *Gauloise*. 'And I do have to agree that the United States does copulate with the European Union. In a broad sense of the term.'

That cracked me up. 'I know nothing about international politics,' I laughed.

'But you do know something about depression, yes? Whill told me you write about your depression,' Charlie said, blowing smoke. 'It is something I have long been dealing with, too. Lady Macbeth went to a doctor for her depression, but he promptly told her there was nothing he could do; it was up to her to make amends with God in order to clear her conscience. Doctors are useless.'

'Really?' I lilted. 'Should you drop to the ground with a heart-attack right now in front of God and everybody, I'll be sure to call your herbalist.'

'You are right, Whill. He is good,' said Roy.

I pulled a sheet of paper from my courior's bag and showed him my brief essay which I had penned over my morning tea.

'This looks very interesting! It's not long. Shall I read it aloud?' he asked. I nodded.

Depression, as an illness of the mind, is not like a disorder of the body where the afflicted can separate himself from the affliction. A broken leg causes suffering, but the pain registered in the mind can be recognized as originating outside the mind – as being extra-mental – and thus as separate from the self. Depression cannot be looked at this way as it is an origination in and of the mind, and even encompasses the mind entirely: the individual is subsumed by the depression and is no longer himself in his own mind. The absorption of the self by the depression is therefore extremely difficult, if not impossible, for the patient to describe to the attending physician. And this difficulty is further aggravated by the pinnacle difference between the treatment of mental illnesses and physical illnesses: a medical doctor can understand the pain of a broken leg; a psychiatrist cannot comprehend the hell of his patient's disorder.

'Not a bad analysis of the situation,' said Charlie.

'Thank you,' I beamed.

'But you write like old people have sex.'

I was hurt. 'I only edited it on the way here, on the metro. I haven't really looked at it closely yet.'

'No matter; you show your inner conflicts well enough. Do you mind if I keep it? I can use it for our next unity roundtable at the *Café de Flore*.'

'Unity roundtable?' I repeated. 'What are you trying to unify?'

'Ah! You miss nothing. The Higher Power and man,' he opined. 'The relationships start there. Man and his philosophy.

Man and his religion. Man and other men. It's all about a higher order of relationships emanating from The Higher Power.'

'You sound like a twelve-step program,' I said.

'It's good unity we care about; as if there were any unity which is not good.' He was looking at Nadya, who was gazing into Charlie's eyes. 'I am parched. Care to get a drink?'

'Relationships and unity with The Higher Power, a noble cause,' I stumbled over myself on the sidewalk. 'Relationships are a noble cause, I mean. A drink would be great, too.'

'Ah ah, Michael,' interjected Nadya. 'You said you stopped drinking.'

I crossed my legs standing there in front of Nadya and Charlie. 'Not all the time,' I lied. 'I gave up drinking hard alcohol. I can have a beer now and then.'

'And after the now and then, you spend the whole next day depressed in bed,' said Nadya.

I scowled. 'Well, I justify it on special occasions.'

'And now is a special occasion,' Charlie diverted. 'We can celebrate our meeting each other. The beginning of a relationship. Come, we drink. Let's walk. The Quiet Man in the Marais is a good place for a pint of Guinness. You do drink, Guinness, don't you, Michael?'

'Guiness is a fine beer,' I replied. 'It's not my favorite, but I could surely enjoy a pint of anything right now.'

'Me, too,' said Charlie. 'I just had a terrible, terrible week.

'How so?' asked Nadya with surprised concern in her voice.

'I sent my cousin Lee back to the U.S. of A. in a casket.'

'NO! REALLY?' Nadya exclaimed.

'Yep. He was here with his wife Agnes visiting me for ten days. They were shopping on *rue St. Honore* late afternoon on Tuesday when Agnes stepped in the Faconnable store for a few minutes; Lee waited outside. She came out a half-hour later to find him all crumpled up on the sidewalk. He had had a heart attack and the damn Parisians had done nothing for him but walk by and step over him for a half-hour! Is that heartless or what? I love this city, but the people kill me. Really they do.'

Charlie grabbed Nadya's elbow and pulled her gently up the street. We were silent as we walked past Notre Dame Cathedral, crossed the Seine river, and passed the *Hotel de Ville* on up the *rue Rivoli* into the Marais. The traffic was heavy and we had to scurry across the *rue Rivoli*, but naturally there were less cars as we entered the *rue du Temple*, the narrow street leading to the center of the Marais. The labrynthian passages of the Marais, with their small cafés and bungalow shops, and cobblestone streets suffering a rash of construction sites, are always charming to the street walker who is not pressed to be anywhere. Charlie pointed out a few doorways where he knew the people who lived in the building: an international model here, a well-known author there, an independent filmmaker nearby.

The Quiet Man wasn't far into the quiet Marais, and I would have blinked and missed the place if Charlie were not with us to point out the entrance. Quaint and unassuming it was. Charlie led Nadya and I up the small steps inside, and we had to squeeze past an older couple with slick hair holding full pints of Guinness and standing by the door; I guess looking for someone else to join them from outside. We pressed through a small crowd of Rugby players (at least that's what they looked like as they had matching red and black jerseys on) to the zinc bar, which wasn't very large itself but took up half of the floor area. I looked around. *I would be surprised if eighteen patrons could enjoy a respite in this bar at one time*, I thought. Not much room but no one seemed to mind being in one another's face. A perfect place for an intimate conversation with a new friend? Well, maybe not perfect, but it would do for now. Elbows bumped me and people stepped on my toes, but I resolved myself to smile and enjoy the physical contact. Every one else there seemed to.

The barkeep had spotted us as we entered and repeatedly made eye contact with Nadya as we made our way up the length of the zinc bar, but he continued his rounds of dart-throwing. We had to wait until he finished, and I noticed that neither Charlie nor Nadya had much to say as we watched with disinterest the darts be thrown. When the squat, red-head barkeep finally gave us service at the bar, Nadya had almost lost her patience and was ready to leave, but Charlie held her hand and ordered us men a pint of Guiness each and Nadya asked for a white-wine spritzer. 'There's no accounting for taste,' Charlie commented. Nadya just winked at him. Charlie led us to a tall table with no stools in the back area by the entrance to the kitchen.

Everyone in the bar was speaking the Queen's English, and we were packed in so tightly that I expected our light philosophical conversation might interest those standing around us to join in, but none did. We were so close together that I had to concentrate on my beer in hand so as not to spill it on Nadya.

'So I ask the aspiring writer... Do you believe in a higher power?' Charlie asked me straight off after we had swallowed a few mouthfulls of beer. 'And if so, where does this belief originate from?'

'My higher power tells me to do the dishes or no sex,' I deadpanned. Neither of my companions laughed. *Tough crowd*, I thought. Maybe this wasn't going to be fun even with ample beer.

Charlie squinted and fingered up a *Gauloise* cigarrette from a crushed pack. 'Whill here tells me you read the Bible and quote it in your works.'

I looked at Nadya. 'I do. But I can't say I rely on it in my writing. I use it anecdotally, just literarilly, really.'

'As if a book could sum up the Higher Power,' said Charlie.

'Don't lead Michael wrong,' Nadya said. 'You know you believe what the Bible says, Charlie.' Charlie smiled and nodded and looked over at me for my thoughts.

'That may be. The Bible does have a beautiful aesthetic that lends itself gracefully to literature. That is why I use it anecdotally,' I offered. 'Really, it is the finest of literature itself.'

Charlie smiled. Nadya just gazed at him. *What is her fascination with Charlie?* I thought to myself.

'The Spanish have a saying: tell me with whom you walk and I will tell you who you are. I say: tell me about your aspirations as a writer and I will tell you who you are,' said Charlie.

'Would you like to read a short story I have written based on a character in the Bible?' I asked cheerfully.

'If you have it with you,' Charlie pointed to my courior bag.

'I do. Here, let me pull it out for you.' I opened my bag and sifted momentarily through the many loose pages and pulled three stapled pages out of a manila folder labeled 'Characters'. Charlie reached to grab it from my hands; I held it back. Before I gave it to him, I wanted him to know a few things.

'First of all,' I said. 'It is in lower-case for a reason, which I hope you will see at the end. And second of all, I expect you to be open and candid with me concerning any and all of your reactions and criticisms to it. Agreed?' I handed it to him slowly.

Charlie nodded sternly and straightened his glasses. 'It's titled *No Small Yield*? I shall read it out loud,' he said.

When Charlie said this, two of the large rugby players turned toward us. Nadya leaned back to invite in the others who may be listening. Charlie took a puff then put down his cigarrette. Here is what Charlie read:

the man strained on his knees, convulsing slightly, his face buried in his hands, waiting. outside the tent the wind blew harshly, sweeping the expansive desert's sand under the fraying edges of the great canvas. the respected elders, five symbols of the cruelty of old age and rigorous labor on the body, sat in a semi-circle with their backs to the wall so as to be seen by, and see, all who entered. directly before them was the man, who dared not raise his countenance, though he did not exude shame. tired men with parched skin and matted hair sat with legs crossed or squatted around him. some, murmuring incoherently, covered their heads with their hairy arms. some clasped their hands tightly and focused intently with their eyes closed. women dressed ornately in fine purple cloths and bare footed pretended to be absorbed in gathering the clay bowls containing uneaten stew. they scurried with caution and in humble silence to avert any remonstration for perceived insolence. knowing that many questions had yet been unanswered, the potentate in the center of the five wanted to continue. he instead signaled the end of the grave discussion by raising a frail and calloused hand and by nodding his head once. the deep furrowing of his bushy white eyebrows indicated to all that no additional insight or wisdom would be necessary that was not already presented. the man's announcement, although bitterly rebuked by all the elders one by one in turn and praised by no other man present, was slowly accepted with determined reservation.

fifteen, maybe twenty, seconds passed, although the time was not recorded, and the man still did not raise his head from his hands. tears that welled up in his eyes streaked down into the uneven stubble on his cheeks. he fought back gut-wrenching sobs. his nails gouged his forehead. the sharp tension in the back of his neck spread lower, forcing him to lower his head more before the magistrates. his biceps hardened to stone. his elbows trembled uncontrollably. gritty perspiration saturated his goat-skin tunic despite the cool evening temperature. though his muscular buttocks cramped, he persisted to hold his position. his tan, hirsute thighs were well flexed, as seen through the bursted course stitching of his tunic. throbbing veins appeared to rupture his finely chiseled calves. every sinew in his seventy-five year-old body was constricted. overrought with conflicting emotions that self-generated from the belly, his mind was unable to override his living flesh, and he collapsed forward. his chest heaved repeatedly; he vomited.

the man had announced his need to leave the village, the very same locale to which his father had brought him, his wife, and his nephew many unrecorded years before. the man's father had led them northwesternly from their homeland following the river on what today we would call an exodus. for an unknown reason, the nomads rested here not reaching the intended destination. they were well accepted by the villagers and the family grew, accumulating great wealth and status. (indeed, we can remark that by his documented geneology and success he was a chosen one among the villagers). but now the man's father had passed away and was buried, and he was suddenly implored to continue his family's exodus.

time was of the essence, which was rare for this era, and the call to leave, however abrupt, entailed imminent consequences if the man tarried. many preparations needed to be completed before setting forth the next dawn. the man's wife was busy preparing their flocks and commanding the servants during the council's meeting. she looked at the expanse of desert beyond the village to the west and sighed, her heart sinking. she was a good, obedient helpmate to her *husband. her only failure was being barren. however deeply she doubted her husband's decision to leave their comfortable home, she accepted unconditionally the word from her master. for inasmuch as she yearned to build a great and powerful family, as all women do, she refused to usurp her spouse's patriarchical authority. bear in mind that she too was of advanced age, but filled with harmonious beauty, and as yet not given to a chastising character. she would be remarked upon later for laughing at faith, but at this moment her zeal for her husband kindled in her the natural melancholic satisfaction of existence.*

no one addressed the man. all moved slowly and silently. three kinsmen helped him carefully to his feet. the youngest of these men was the man's nephew, previously mentioned. stern, reflective, but with a faint, crisp smile, the nephew placed his hands on the torso of his pious uncle, appearing outwardly to brace his mentor, but knowing inwardly that he was drawing and radiating strength. to describe this humble nephew as loyal to his uncle would be to show the sun with a candle. he looked upon his graying teacher not with inconsiderate awe but with honorable introspection. not much is known further about their familial relationship at this time in history, but we do know that the man regarded his nephew closely, not as a son, but rather as a brother. brothers, being the only male kin from their ancestry in this region, and brotherhood, born from past and continuing adversity, seeking blindly together the way towards internal freedom.

many experiences had passed through the man's life, some mundane, others eventfull. never had his soul been so drained and subsequently renewed of strength. never had he failed to realize his mortality and the necessity for responsibility. his life was simple, and he new nothing more complex than to do justly and to love mercy. but now the concrete world he knew would become mere memories. his spiritual foundation would be broken, to be built anew. with a few steps towards the exit of the tent he summoned the languishing internal light that first incited him to enter. the wind settled to a wimper, his mind emptied, and he felt an invigorating energy reach the extremeties of his body. asssurance and comfort came to his soul. after a pause he lapsed free of the hands that steadied him. somberly and with a distinct aura he strode with his nephew beside him through the village while softly discoursing on the guiding heavens and pondering enthusiastically the gradual revelation of the Almighty.

and yet----well… you can read the rest of his story in Genesis 12.
yes, Yahweh called. and abram obeyed.

'That's it,' Charlie finished.

'Well, what did you think of it,' I asked curiously. The rugby players turned back to their grungy group without comment.

Charlie paused a second. 'You are forbidden to have fun, aren't you, Michael? It's a religious thing for you, isn't it?'

I was perplexed. 'Why do you say that?' I murmured, trying to hide my confusion.

'You know, Michael.'

He waited for me to answer. I said nothing.

'You know, I haven't known you but for the past ninety minutes. But there is something I have to tell you.'

'Oh, really?' I asked with disdain, presuming he wanted to trash the story. Or worse, trash my love for writing.

A look of concern like a grandparent has for a child came to his wrinkled old face. 'Michael, Michael, Michael. You are not perfect. You are human,' he said, taking a puff from his *Gauloise*. 'A closed fist and a closed heart both hold darkness. But open them both up and the darkness disappears.'

'That's it?! That's all you have to tell me?' I was indeed hurt. 'Do you really think I don't know that?'

'You are not perfect. And more importantly for you to understand, you don't have to be.'

I looked at Nadya. She looked at me and nodded.

'I don't understand. This really isn't what I was expecting for comments.'

'God has His ways. Ways known and unknown to man.' Charlie put down his cigarrette and placed his hand softly on mine which was resting on the table. He looked into my eyes, into me, like he had known me and my soul and my spirit for more than the ages. 'Put away your Bible. God loves you and I know you love God. But God cannot make you love yourself any more than He can make you love Him. You alone have the choice to love yourself. And you know something? I don't think you do.'

'But? But?'

Chapter IX

After Charlie's comments, the conversation with Charlie and Nadya did not last much longer, and I really had the urge to run away and hide from everything and all that I was responsible for. We said our goodbyes, promising to meet again soon for more drinks and chat on the meaning in, about, and of life. I walked alone back out into the drizzle, got on the metro and headed towards the *Etoile*. What Charlie said to me really struck a nerve. I was hurt. It was time for more alcohol. *Yes, I want some alcohol.* What else could I do to dull the pain of what Charlie had said? Julia wouldn't be home. Maybe I should just go home and take a nap. The bed would be comfortable. All I needed was to get a full bottle for a pillow and be a lush.

On the way walking from *Etoile* towards *Pereire* and towards home, I stopped at an Arab corner store to find and buy a bottle of something, anything, that had liquor in it. Arab stores seldom carry a good mark when it comes to alcohol, but if you are lucky one might have the off, random bottle of something really good at a bargain price. I can spend a good twenty or thirty minutes looking at bottles of whatever is for sale in the Arab stores – kind of like a treasure hunt. In this one I stopped in, I mused a long while over the expansive shelves of hard alcohols and spotted a bottle of Malibu Jamaican Rum for eight Euro, not a bad deal.

But as I reached for the bottle on the shelf, the proprietor came up to me holding a dusty bottle of Havana Club Rum *Especial*. He literally shoved it into my face as if to say *here, take this, it's much better than that crap you have in your hand.* When I inquired about the price, letting him know that I had only a ten Euro note and some *sou* with me because I had left my *carte blue* at home by mistake, he told me that I could have it for the same price as the Malibu, eight Euro.

Eight Euro for a bottle of Havana Club! A delicious rum not found in the U.S. due to the trade embargo with Fidel Castro? Authentic Hemingway sipping liquor! What a find! Today would not turn out to be so bad after all.

I took the bottle, skipped to the front of the store, stopping to pick up a plastic bottle of Coca-Cola Light, and set the bottles of rum and cola on the counter.

'*Ten-fifty*', said the pear-shaped woman with a pocked face from behind the counter.

'*How much is the Coca-Cola Light?*' I inquired.

'*One-twenty-five,*' she said impatiently.

'*But the bottle of rum is only eight Euro,*' I countered, pointing to the proprietor, now standing in the doorway. '*He told me so.*'

A harsh argument ensued between the woman and the man in a language I could not identify, and there I stood, nervously hoping the man would win and I could have my good bottle of Cuban rum at such a discount. But alas, it was not to be my way this time, as the man waved an arm and gave up.

The woman gave me a cheshire-cat grin. I laid my solitary ten Euro note on the counter and pulled a fifty *sou* from my coin bag. The woman put my purchases in a paper bag and stepped back to her television soap opera. I looked at the proprietor as I walked out; he just smiled weakly and shrugged.

Really I wondered as I walked away if I was not set up to pay the higher price in the first place. That would not have surprised me, being cheated by such Parisian social lowlife.

It was not my first run in with Muslims in Paris, as just a few weeks earlier Olivier and I took a cab from *Le Chat Noir* in search of late-night munchies and the hairy, oily driver, who had Quran scripture on the back of his seat for all passengers to read in French and Arabic, tried to overcharge us- probably thinking we were tourists. When Olivier protested in perfect Arabic, the driver snapped at him and told him to go home to his whore-mother (at least that is what Olivier told me later he said). There was nothing we could do about this situation since we had asked to be taken to *Barbes-Rochechouart* to go to our favorite cheap eatery for some *merguez* sausage sandwiches and fries, and as any Parisian knows – and thus avoids - *Barbes* is the heart of the Muslim area. If we had protested too loudly, we might have been jumped and beaten up. *Thank be to God Julia is not with us for this encounter*, I thought at the time.

On another bad occasion with a North African, Julia and I had just seen a movie in *St. Denis* at the discount theater when we stopped to eat some Greek sandwiches and fries in a greasy dive. When the waiter brought us incorrect change, I calmly asked him if he could recount the bill and what we paid.

'*I counted correctly. Where you from?*' the waiter asked me gruffly.

'*The United States,*' I replied.

'*I must be just some dumb-ass from Algeria for you, no?*' he said sarcastically.

'*What do I know?*' I said pretending to be stupid. '*You might be a dumb-ass from anywhere.*'

I am not racist, and I will say one thing for Muslim men: they know how to keep their wives and daughters at home and out of trouble. And they also know how to keep their mistresses a fair distance away from their wives. A Muslim man can have four wives, according to the Quran. Muhammed, the Prophet, had more than ten wives, one of whom was only ten years old when he married her.

But I digress.

Now this day with a bottle of good rum in hand, much needed after Charlie's painful comments, I was going home to drink and sleep until I would see my future wife – the Chosen One – who loved me. That was all that mattered.

As soon as I walked through the door, Julia met me with a big kiss.

'Uh, hello. I didn't expect you to be home,' I said nervously, trying to hide the rum behind my back.

'Dat girl, Nadya, she call you, *Meeko*.'

'Thanks, baby,' I looked at her lustfully. 'Did you have a good day?'

'No bad. I talk with my mama, and she tell me papa is back in the hospital. Problems with his kidneys again. Why he don't take his medicines?'

'Your father is a great man. You know I love him so.'

'Yes, I know this. Now I going to Montparnasse. I am in hurry. My client, she wants her hair-do done. Kiss kiss?'

I kissed Julia, and she bounded down the six levels of stairs leaving me standing with my bottles in the doorway of the apartment.

In less than a second, the phone rang. It was Nadya; could I buzz her in? I poked the buzzer and I heard the downstairs door open. Nadya and Julia exchanged pleasantries and Nadya came up the stairs.

'Michael, you left Charlie and I rather quickly,' she said frowning. 'You didn't enjoy our company?'

I replied that yes, I enjoyed the company, but that I was hurt at what Charlie said about me not loving myself.

'There are none so blind as those who will not see,' Nadya focused on me. 'Charlie told me to tell you that.'

'Well good for Charlie. Let's go sit and have a drink.'

'Okay,' said Nadya. I was surprised she said yes to a hard-alcohol drink.

I pulled some mismatched glasses from the cabinet and placed them on the dining room table. I opened the rum and smelled the cooled liquid inside.

'Mmmm!' I said. 'Nothing better than Cuban rum. Can't get this fine stuff in the States. Trade embargo and all. Castros' best I offer you, my dear.'

Nadya took the bottle from my hands and poured a few shots worth into each glass. Was she going to drink all that rum, I asked, and did she want some Coca Light for mixer? I did not have to wait for an answer as she downed the half-full glass and pushed the other one to me. What could I do? I opened my gullet and downed the other glass.

'Mmmmm. Smooth,' I said. 'What are you thinking?'

'Charlie asked me to give you his card. If you call him, he will meet you at the Hemingway Bar. It's in the Ritz Hotel. Next Saturday at 3pm. Can you go?' She handed a calling card to me. All it had printed on it was *Charlie...Scholared Artiste... Paris...33.1.46.24.38.77.*

'I'm not going to the Hemingway Bar. I hear it is too damn expensive.'

'Don't worry about that. Charlie will pay, of course.'

'He will? And how can Charlie afford that?'

'He is rich!' Nadya exclaimed. 'Funny thing, because he says men don't seek to be rich, but only to be richer than other men.'

'So you say. Just to be curious as any bold American is, how did he make his money?'

'You ever hear of Miro?'

'Miro? Joan Miro? The artist?'

'The same. Charlie brought him baguettes and cheese when he was a starving painter up on *Montmartre* during the Nazi occupation.'

'And for that Charlie got some of his works in return? Really?' I asked incredulously.

'Charlie's father actually. He owned a Paris art gallery before they moved to the States after the war. Many of Miro's early works went with them to the U.S. in those years.'

'Damn. He must be loaded then.'

'Terribly so. But he never lets on, no?'

I shook my head. 'Never would have guessed. That ill-fitting suit he was wearing was crap.'

Nadya poured two more shots worth into each of our glasses. We downed them laughing.

'Why are you drinking so much?' I asked. 'You never drink. Not that I am complaining that the liquor is flowing.'

She batted her eyelashes.

'This rum is so good!' I exclaimed, pouring again.

'Michael, do you think I am attractive?' Nadya asked coyly.

'Well, actually I do,' I tried to be diplomatic. 'But you are always taken by some man greater than I.'

'You don't think I am attractive. You have never tried to kiss me.'

Kissing a prostitute? Nasty, I thought.

She crossed her legs at the knee. 'I saw Julia on her way out. She looks good. Quite attractive today.'

I could tell she wanted me to comment; somehow she would find a tasty tidbit of information to use to her favor. What did she want? I kept silent.

'Don't you want to kiss me?'

'Where did Charlie go after I left? And why did you come here?' I asked, feeling the alcohol and nervousness suddenly hit me like a rushing waterfall.

'Michael, I asked you a question.'

''Nother drink?' I started to pour some of the rum into the two glasses.

'Michael, you ran off so quickly from Charlie and me and now you are offending my sensibilities.'

'Sorry, I didn't mean to do that. You know I love my Julia, Nadya. By the way, why does Charlie call you Whill?'

'It means *the other woman* in the Indonesian language.'

'You mean you and Charlie?'

She arched an eyebrow.

I needed something other than straight rum, even one as tasty as the Havana Club. I poured some Coca Light into the glass of rum and swallowed a stretch.

'Whill, I mean Nadya, I can't kiss you,' I looked down into my empty glass. 'It would change our friendship. And really I am so in love with my Julia.'

'You can't kiss me because of Julia? You aren't married to her.'

'But we are living together and we are for all practicality engaged to be married- someday.'

'Why be with just one girl? You can have so many more. You Americans are such Puritans. Live a little, like Charlie told you.'

I felt a foot under the table slide up my leg. We just looked into each others' eyes.

I poured again, and took a quick drink, crouching my arms on the table defensively. She laughed softly and tickled my crotch.

I stood up. 'Nadya I can't do this. I am sorry.'

She frowned then drank from her glass. 'Well then, excuse me a minute. Can I use your WC?' she asked.

'It's in the hallway just past the next apartment's door,' I pointed.

Nadya went out, closing the door behind her. I waited.

I went to the freezer and cracked some ice to drop into the glasses. I poured some more rum into my glass without Coca Light and took a straight drink. Wow, it tasted so good. And the thought of being miserably passed out when Julia would come home did not stop me from drinking more. What was Nadya up to? She never acted so boldly like this before. This was a new experience for us both. And she did look good in the sundress she was wearing, her long mocha legs and bright brown eyes with long eyelashes.

I sat to rest in my wearied, brain-diluted state. I waited. Still Nadya did not return. I waited for a while longer then got up to go look in the hallway. The door to the watercloset was open and Nadya was nowhere to be seen. Just then the phone rang. I stumbled back into the apartment to answer it; I fumbled it on the floor.

'*Allo, Meeko?*'

'Yesh, baby.'

'Are you busy? I saw your friend come in. Is she still there? Can you run down to the butcher's and pick up the- *Meeko*, you are breathing heavy. You sound very drunkness on the phone. Are you drinking?'

I kept silent.

'Please get the *pate de campagne* and the duck for dinner. We gonna eat well tonight with the tip I get from my client this morning! I already pay the butcher. You can ask your friend to join us if you are wanting. Is she still there? I am too busy now, and the butcher will to close soon. So be a dear and go pick up the *pate* and the duck. I think the butcher overcharged me for the duck. Can you to ask him the price? I am sure he charge me too much, *Meeko*. We can call my mama again tonight after dinner, no? I am worry about my father. Why he don't take his medicines? Oh, and your brother, David, he call you. He say he hope you feeling much better now. *Meeko*, are you drinking too much again?... *Meeko*? Are you crying. Why you crying, *Meeko*? Why you crying, I say?...'

Chapter X

Nadya called meone soul-chilling, depressing evening a few days later to apologize for her behavior on Saturday and thank me for the rum drinks. When I said I would accept her apology if she would tell me why she was drinking so much lately, she changed the topic quickly to ask me if I still was planning to meet Charlie the upcoming weekend for drinks at the Heminway Bar.

'Hadn't realized I agreed to that yet,' I said. 'I don't know, Nadya. I was kind of fired this week because I missed so many days last month due to my depression. My Julia hasn't been pulling the tips either, because it's slow at the salon. Not good. We don't have much money right now.'

'Charlie will pay for lunch, I tell you,' said Nadya. 'And he really wants to talk to you. He can't stop gushing on and on about your writings. Rarely is he so taken with someone's talent. So feel special. Go on, take a chance and meet with him *mono a mono*. You have only to profit from knowing him. *D'accord?*'

'Okay. *D'accord*,' I agreed. 'I don't know why I am accepting his kind offer, though, after he hurt me. Who the hell is he to tell me I don't love myself?'

'There are none so blind as those who will not see.'

'So you told me,' I said dryly. 'I'll call you after mass on Sunday, if I feel good enough to go to *Notre Dame*. My depression is killing me. Tell Charlie if he really wants to meet me and buy me drinks, I am gonna tie one on. I am in that mood to be a drunk.'

'He expects nothing less.'

And so it went that I spent the rest of the days that drizzly week depressed, alone, unemployed, waiting for *le weekend* and the sun to arrive for a reason to take my sorry self out of bed to meet Charlie for a drink- if not just long enough for Julia to change the bedsheets and vacuum. Nothing is a noiser hell to someone with depression than a French vacuum. And Julia was sick enough of me and my complaining by the weekend's coming that Saturday noon she angrily took out the vacuum and fired it up next to the bed. What could I do? I got myself up, put on my best sports coat, and left unshaven and unshowered to go meet Charlie at the Hemingway Bar.

Not a bad day outside. The sun peeked out of the gray clouds and shined down like a gift from heaven above. I took the metro to *Tuileries* and walked up *rue Rivoli* passing by Angelina's, one of my mother's favorite places in Paris. Angelina's is well known for its Belle Epoque decor and delicious *Chocolat a l'Africain* – hot chocolate that is so thick and rich that you can scoop it out of the *demitasse* with a teaspoon. And it goes without saying that there must be included rich, whipped cream with the hot chocolate, which Angelina's serves limitlessly- enough fat to destroy even an Ethiopian marathon-runner's gall bladder.

I stood a moment in front of Angelina's looking at the line of refined people of all ages (definitely not tourists) waiting to get in. The wind was blowing and the air was cooled under the building canopy, but this did not stop these well-groomed people who, some with their pet dogs to join them, were willing to bundle up and wait all afternoon to partake of an unforgettable midday Marie-Antoinette-affair that only Angelina's offers for an unduly reasonable price. Francois Mitterand's mistress, for one, was known to have frequented this location on a regular basis. Oh, how I enjoyed that locale, with its guilded molding and expansive mirrors – not to mention the finely appointed waiters in tuxedos - on several occasions! But my Julia was not with me now, and I was headed for an entirely different affair. Angelina's would have to wait.

Right next to Angelina's is the Hotel Meurice, a well-bred spot where the actor Robert de Niro respites during his stays in Paris. Out front of this fine hotel there was parked the requisite new, fire-engine red Ferrari in the reserved valet spot. *Probably Robert de Niro's ride while he's here*, I thought to myself. *If not for his great roles, I could really learn to hate de Niro.*

This fancy hotel, too, I passed by.

A short amble on and I was turning left at *rue Castigilioni* which led towards *Place Vendome*. There I was, right in the heart of *Place Vendome*, which, with its many swanky jewelry stores, held little that could include a nobody like me. It was at this point in my walk when I started to feel uncomfortable about what I was wearing and how I looked. *What if they don't let me in the hotel?* I thought. *I should have worn the one good suit I possess. I wonder what Charlie will be wearing. Why does it matter, anyway? Does it really matter at all what we wear in life?*

A few steps more and I was at the front of the Paris-Ritz Hotel, at 38 *rue Cambon*, stopping to take in a view of the prim and proper entrance to a finely attuned lifestyle at its best.

I walked up to the glass doors of the Ritz and saw in there all the high-humanity with its otherwise unassuming glory moving about the reception area and concierge desk like a swarm of bees surrounding a hive. My own nervousness was welling up inside me, but outwardly I managed to keep it hidden. *Why should I show others I don't belong here?* I thought to myself. *If not for the uniforms, I surely couldn't distinguish the bellhops from the guests.* That was my own lack of knowledge about refined society at the time. A long time later, I would learn differently. *The rich are not like you and I,* said Fitzgerald to Hemingway. *Yes,* replied Hemingway. *They have more money.*

How should I act? If I could act like I belonged there, then it must be true that I did belong there. After all, they were not going to throw me out, were they? They did not know me or my history of depression. If they did, would they ask me to leave, charging me with upsetting the other clientelle? I was meeting someone and he knew the place well, probably even knows the hotel manager well, and if he wanted me to come meet him there, then I must belong there. Should I walk in with my nose in the air? Should I avoid the eyes of people in the lobby, or smile and nod to them as if I were a regular patron? I did not have long to worry because right by the reception desk and concierge I went without mind, and no one noticed me. All I had to do was continue to pretend I knew well where I was and what I was doing. How difficult was that? And I would be getting some alcohol- drinks in the Hemingway Bar after all. What is there better in Paris for a writer than to drink where Hemingway and and the best of authors past drank? If I played my game right, this day would turn out to be one for the books. No worries!

The famous and infamous Hemingway Bar is well-hidden, I decided, for a reason. Here the still-today reviled Vichy Government held its own opulent air with the German generals. Government, Germans, jewelry, women, alcohols, extreme prices- all provoke and disallow for secrecy. A hidden bar, for all its purposes, was inexhorably a necessity.

My destination, the bar, is at the far end of the Ritz, past crowded and winding hallways. Boldly I strutted past the excellently appointed footmen, who were ingratiatingly serving the wealthy all around me. I came upon what seemed to be an opening to a small nook. *This is it? How unassuming!* I walked through the miniature entrance into the bar and looked around. Charlie was not yet there. Oh, oh. I am alone. Disheveled and non-plussed was I. Not good.

Why was I meeting Charlie here and not at some more palpable spot where I could blend in, like the Cafe des Ecoles or Cafe Beaubourg? I questioned myself. My mind settled on only one answer: I was wanting to see the locale where my favorite author, Hemingway, wined and dined regularly with gusto when he became the foremost worldly writer among writers of the world. And maybe, if the muses were with me, I could get his inspirations for my own writings.

I collected myself. Look at those finely wood-panneled walls! I had never been in such a fancy bar as this. *This room is the epitome of perfection*, I thought. *Even the bar looks perfect and gloss, like it has never been used..*

A soul-simmering jealousy rose inside my gut as I glanced dismissively at the other guests, all dressed up in their Saturday's finest clothing and jewelry, and me here in my faded khaki pants; the ones Julia told me not to wear; the ones she wanted to throw away. Julia always knew something I did not. One of the reasons I loved her so.

Well, I thought. *Hemingway liberated the Ritz from the Nazis on August 25, 1944. That was one of Hemingway's moments. Life comes down to a few moments; this is one for moi.*

So I stepped from blocking the entrance up to the glossed bar and sat myself down comfortably on one of the padded, leather bar stools. *Do I look like I belong here? I wish my Julia were with me. Damn, my shoes are scuffed.* I noticed all the pictures of Hemingway on the walls. What a man he was. *Why can't I be a real man like Hemingway?*

A few minutes passed and still no sign of Charlie, and even worse, no sign of a barkeep. *What kind of place is this?* I postured. *The other guests have drinks. Does a bartender only show himself for the well-monied guests?* I had to wait for Charlie anyway; he was to be the one who pays. I waited quietly, looking at the rows of alcohols behind the bar and mixing various cocktails in my mind.. After about ten or twelve impatient minutes, a barkeep showed.

'*M'sieu?*'

I stammered.

Noticing my immediate nervousness, he smiled and started to speak to me in English. 'Would *m'sieu* care for something from zee bah?'

'Ummm.'

Patiently, the barkeep raised his eyebrows and smiled, and waited on me to decide.

'Ummm. *Cuba libre.*'

'Top shelf?'

'Yeah. I mean, thank you, yes.'

The barkeep nodded knowingly, looked briskly at the rows of alcohols receded against the wall, then turned and headed to the backroom for a moment.

Why did you say yes to top shelf? Idiot! That drink is going to cost Charlie big time! And what if, God forbid, he doesn't show? How many Euro do you have in your pocket anyway? Maybe eight; maybe ten? You should have gone to an ATM machine before coming here!

The barkeep returned carrying a full bottle of Anejo Gold rum. I was not able to discern what make – I had never seen it before - but the bottle itself certainly looked elegant. In a few moments of graceful preparation by the barkeep, the *Cuba Libre* was in a highball glass before me on a white, Ritz-embossed, cocktail napkin. I stared at the drink.

A minute later and I was still starting at the drink.

'Ees there ay problem with zee drink, *m'sieu*?'

'Uh, no. No. No problem, my good man,' I sat up straight. 'Thank you.'

The bartender nodded politely and went to the backroom.

Well, Michael, do you drink it or just sit and look at it?

Another of life's fine moments. Me, sitting in the Paris-Ritz – the Hemingway Bar after all! - with a finely prepared *Cuba Libre* ready to be imbibed. I had arrived. Time to savor the moment. I picked up the cold glass.

'Good for you, chum, I see you started without me.'

'Wha-?' *CRASH!*

I had dropped the drink on the inlaid hardwood bar. Rum and cola spilled all over the counter and my faded khaki pants. 'SHIT!' I yelled.

It was Charlie, and he started to laugh heartily.

'SHIT and DAMN IT!' I said a few times. A curious smile came to the barkeep as he rushed in from the backroom. He handed me a few cloth napkins to dry myself. A barback also came in from the backroom after hearing the commotion. He grabbed a wet cloth and wiped the bar down. The barback and the keep exchanged a few words in low voices. I was mortified.

'Glad to see you made it, chum,' said Charlie. 'It's okay. It happens. Have a seat and we will order some drinks together. We can even ask for extra napkins for you, if you think you will need them.'

I shook my head with my face falling low.

Charlie laughed. 'You are beet red, Michael. Have a seat. Let's drink to today and to the good Lord above, shall we? What are you drinking anyway? I hope it wasn't just Coca-cola in that glass you dropped.'

The bartender brought me another drink, and I guess he and Charlie knew each other pretty well because he brought

Charlie his drink without him asking for it. I figured I could relax and enjoy my *Cuba Libre* now that Charlie was here to join me. I could not tell what he was drinking, however, and I was curious.

'Michael, Michael, Michael. We have so much in common, you and I. I was right where you are now oh-so-many years ago. A day after Paris was liberated, my father was to meet me here to celebrate the victory. I was sitting right over there with a lovely daughter of the Underground, and both of us watched as Ernest Hemingway and Irwin Shaw got boiled like lobsters over lunch and French 75's. Do you know what goes in a well-made French 75? Gin, sugar, fresh lemon juice, and a topping off of good champagne. Of course I did not have much money then, or I pretended not to – I forget - so the girl and I couldn't drink those; we drank the cheapest vodka. Do you know why vodka is still considered a woman's drink? Because it doesn't show on the breath, and women used to drink it when it was considered uncivilized for them to drink alcohol. Bet you didn't know that did you?'

I shook my head.

'You don't speak much, Michael.'

I shrugged. 'If I cannot speak with perfection in my words, like you, why speak at all?'

Charlie smiled. He patted my hand. 'Yes, I know you. Conciliatory by nature. But underneath that niceness is a boiling pot of lava. And you need to let it out.'

'So my therapist tells me.'

He squinted. 'Therapists, you say? Yes. Useless. Remember what I told you about Lady Macbeth; the best doctor couldn't help her, and he knew it. Let's have a drink. A toast?'

We clinked glasses.

Charlie looked into my eyes, the windows of my soul. 'Michael, I know what is troubling you, yes, I do, and I want you to know that it wasn't your fault. Nadya told me everything. Your father was a helpless man, and dare I say it without you slugging me, he was a coward.'

This took me aback. A coward? *What the hell?* How could he say that about my father? My father a coward? *A--hole!* He had hurt me again, this guy! My opinion of Charlie dived at that moment. I wanted to leave right then and there. To hell with the famous Hemingway Bar! To hell with my *Cuba Libre*! And to hell with Charlie!

I swallowed my drink whole – nearly choking on the coldness – and stood up to leave. Charlie put his hand on my shoulder.

'It's okay to drink, alcohol will help to ease the pain you are in- for the moment. More work on your part is needed. First, just accept that there is a heaven, and your father is there. That is not me talking lightheartedly. That is God's promise to you.'

I took a step to the side as I did not want to see his face. I turned to look out the window. Paris suddenly seemed less inviting. How I hated myself at that moment.

Charlie continued. 'A Monarch butterfly must struggle in pain until it comes out of its coccoon. A mother must suffer through long labor until her child is born. But once these two ugly acts of nature are complete, there is beauty in the world. Many great men have had to suffer in life before becoming great men. And I foresee you becoming a great man someday, Michael.'

I did not move except to take Charlie's hand off my shoulder.

'You have to accept that it wasn't your fault, what your father did. He made his own choice. It doesn't matter that you had a fight with him and his girlfriend the night before he committed suicide. How can a twelve year old boy affect a grown man in such a way? A boy can't. Do you hear me? *Cannot!* The grown man makes his own choices. Your father could have gotten help for his problems if he wanted to. He chose not to. It was his struggle. That isn't your fault. What is your fault is you are carrying that pain still today. That is not what Jesus wants for you. He wants you to be free. Satan wants to keep you in pain. Do you hear me?'

'I didn't have to tell him he didn't love me that night,' I said softly, looking down. 'I caused him too much pain late in his life. I fought with my brothers and sisters too much and he couldn't handle it. I told him he loved Kitty's son, Joey, more than he loved me. It wasn't right to say that.'

'You fought with your brothers and sisters and you think that is why he killed himself? Do you really think that?'

'I don't know, I guess.'

'Michael, be free of this pain. Let it go. No therapy in the world, and no person is going to be able to take that pain from you. Indeed, even Jesus can not take the pain away until you give it up freely. Why are you so hard on yourself?'

Tears were welling in my eyes. 'I don't know how to be any other way, Charlie. It isn't fair I have this burden, but I still believe it to be my fault. It was my fault. It was!'

Charlie sat me down gently.

I had my head in my hands. 'Please can I have another drink?'

'Rum isn't going to help your tomorrows. Don't use it that way.'

I started sobbing.

'Oh, Michael. Feel the pain and let it go.' He tried to hug me. I wasn't going to let him hug me here, not in front of the many pictures of my favortie hero and writer on the wall.

I cried and cried, and I was unsure if the other guests were aware or oblivious, but I could not have cared either way.

'Let's wait until you calm down.'

'I don't want to be like this. Not any more. I have had it. I don't know what to do with my life. I hate everything.'

Charlie laughed softly. 'I know you don't hate *everything*, now. You love your Julia, right?'

I raised my head and nodded.

'And you love your writing, right?'

I nodded. 'But it doesn't pay me anything.'

'We can work on that. But I have bigger plans for you. Jesus has bigger plans for you.'

I straightened up and pulled a hankie from my vest pocket and wiped my face.

'Go wash yourself and come back. We will enjoy each other's company here and now. Go on. The loo is over there. Go ahead and wash yourself.' He waved a hand at me.

I went to the washroom, and what a washroom it was! Octagon mirrors over the basins. Very classy. I could not imagine a better place to wash my face and relieve myself. When I came back, Charlie was talking with the bartender.

'Zees ees zee lad you menshoned to mee, Shar-lee?' asked the bartender.

'Yes', said Charlie. 'He is going to be a big man someday. He just doesn't know it yet.'

'*Eh, bien.* Very well!' The barkeep smiled at me and walked to the other room.

'You look better,' said Charlie. 'Now have a seat. Pierre left a full bottle for us behind the counter. We just take it as we want. But we aren't going to depend on it. Okay?'

'Thanks, Charlie. I am feeling better.'

'We have to discuss your future, my friend. And first things first. Your Julia, you love her right?'

I nodded. 'Very much. Very much besotted am I.'

'Then why don't you marry her?'

'We plan to, but that is not gonna happen until we are back in the States. Or maybe in Peru, if-'

'Nonsense. Why wait? You can marry her here in Paris! Wouldn't that be wonderfully romantic?'

'I guess I am too afraid.'

'That is because of your relationship with your mother.'

'Why aren't you married?' I queried.

'Because I am always to wander the earth like Cain. Don't look at me as an example. You are far too fine a person.'

'When we go back to the States-'

'Why wait?' Charlie smiled.

'Getting married in Paris would be romantic, and enchanting!'

'Well, I'll have to talk to Julia about it.'

'No need. I already have,' he said with a glint in his eye. 'It is a done deal.'

'YOU WHAT?!' I demanded.

'I spoke with Julia. Yesterday on her cell phone. I asked her if she would marry you. And she said yes! So…congratulations, *Meeko*.'

Meeko? He had talked to Julia! I was dumbfounded. Who was this guy to talk to my Julia? And about marriage of all things!

'She is working on the details with the *Mairie* as we speak. But I ask one thing of you: be careful of Julia or any other woman for that matter. Remember, Adam's rib was crooked, and it can't in any way possible be straightened. Many men have tried, only to fail miserably. Now onto other things.'

'But…but…' I protested.

'Yes, other things. Like your career. You like teaching, yes?'

'Yes, but-'

'Then I want you to teach people to love others, in your way, just as *you* love others.'

'I don't know how to do that, Charlie. What do I teach?'

'Easy. You just start off by being a fruit inspector. Do you understand what that means?'

I shook my head.

'It means you look at the fruit of anything another person believes, says, or does. And if the fruit is wholesome and beautiful, then you teach that. You inspect the fruit – the result and consequences- of the action of another. If the consequences add benefit and beauty to life, then the content becomes your teaching material. Got it?'

'Give me an example,' I pressured him.

'You like the Bible. You read 1 Corinthians 13. Written by whom? Paul. What does it say? *If I give all I have to the poor, but have not love, then I am worthless.* You have to teach people to give, yes, but there is a condition. In that giving there must be… love! There are many beliefs, ideologies, doctrines, and dogmas. All say you must give. None teach about giving only in love. You cannot help a person see Jesus, but you can help a person see love. You show Jesus in you in love to others, Michael, I know you very well. Now go and spread that knowledge about how to love in Jesus' name and give to others.'

'Charlie, you haven't touched your drink,' I tried to change the subject.

'Never mind the alcohol. Do you know what it takes to be a follower of Christ?'

'No. No, I guess I don't.'

'People followed Jesus as long as He fed them and cared for them. But once He spoke about Himself being the Messiah, saying that you have to drink His Blood and eat His Flesh, many deserted Him. Can you imagine Jesus telling that to a Jewish rabbi 2,000 years ago? Drink His Blood? Eat His Flesh? No wonder so many disciples left Him at that instance.'

'Why are you telling me this?' I queried.

'The world is unsaved and needs help. You can help the world, Michael. Do you believe me? Lead men to salvation. Lead them. You cannot save them. But you can lead them.' There were those creased eyes again, looking into my soul. How nervous, he made me. 'All religions but one have men looking for God. Christianity is God looking for man. Look at the fruit. Christendom has brought great hospitals and other social services and civility, and making that happen are devout, honorable men and women of medicine and

87

science and letters. No other religion can boast that. It's what makes Western Civilization so powerful: Judeo-Christianity. And Western Civilization is self-destructing miserably as we speak.'

I just stood there, wondering what he would say next to bowl me over.

'So that leads me to the next thing I want you to work on: your country. My country. Everyone's country. The world's only superpower. Michael, you have to save America. The greatest power the world has ever seen is in decline.'

'I'm not sure I-'

'F. Scott Fitzgerald once said that there are no second acts in American lives. Well, this Bush Administration is going to prove that wrong. You will bring America back to greatness by your love for others the world over.'

'That is an awfully tall order,' I asserted.

'One last thing, Michael. And this is important; you will remember this long after I am gone from your life. And that is: have faith in no man. That you must accept. You will be alone in life, as all hardworking men of Christ are. Only Jesus will be with you. Can you handle that? It will be for your entire life- to be alone. Of course, your Julia will be there for you, but no man will ever care for you. Not even your son, if you have one. *For momentary, light affliction is producing in us an eternal weight of glory.'*

Down my drink went- to the bottom of my gullet. I reached for the bottle behind the bar. Don-Q rum, it was. Classy. I poured myself a full glass, no mixer. At this Charlie shook his head gently but took a short swig of his drink as well.

'You have little to say, I know. But someday all that I am telling you will make good sense. Now, it is time for you to leave, as I am soon meeting Marcel here.'

'Marcel? You mean Marcel Marceau? Nadya told me you know him.'

'The same. Do you know his real name? Marcel Mangel. He changed his name when he was with the Resistance. His father went to Auschwitz. Don't you think losing his father and family to the Nazis he fought was painful for him?'

'All that pain,' I said softly.

'Yes, all that pain. And look at the beauty he brought to the world. The struggle to become a butterfly. Come now. I will walk you outside through the maddening crowd that is the Ritz."

Charlie and I walked out of the bar, through the hotel, and out into the clear, sunny day on *rue Cambon*, shocking me back to reality, ending my rum buzz.

'Charlie, you have done so much for me today. I feel that I owe you something. Is there anything at all I can do for you? Anything at all?'

'Why, yes. Yes, there is, Michael. Yes,' he replied.

'What is it?' I asked excitedly.

'You are blocking my sunlight.'

Chapter XI

The second to last day I would be in Paris started off with my realizing that I had too much to do to ensure that my and Julia's leaving would be smooth. But packing and cleaning on my last day? The sun was shining, and I was feeling too good for that! I had to get out into the sunshine. Julia knowing well my yearning to be free sent me to spend the better part of the morning at the France Telecom office near *Place Ternes* returning the rented phone and canceling the service. Why was I leaving Paris, the clerk at the phone office asked me. I told her I realized my personal problems weren't going to be solved so far away from my family, and that my fiance, Julia, and I had run out of money and needed to get paying jobs back in the States. Would we be living in New York City, she asked. I shook my head no. She just shook her head in return, as if to say *nothing like Paris can be found in America, my friend, except maybe New York City*. Many would agree.

When I got back to the apartment, Julia was busy packing up the last of the odds and ends and rearranging the apartment so as to leave it clean and organized for Madame Juneot, the landlady. I opened a Coca-Cola Light and sat at the table.

'Meeko,' Julia said from the other room. 'Dat girl, Nadya, called you. She says she will be at the *St.Michel* fountain at 1p.m.'

'Do you mind if I go, Julia? I mean, I don't want to leave you here alone to do all the work.'

'Please go, Meeko. I will finish here without you. But I want you back for dinner. I want to spend our last night in Paris at the *Sacre Coeur* praying for my parents.'

I stuffed an unopened can of Orangina into my courior bag, kissed Julia goodbye, and ran down the stairs into the sunshine and the open crowds walking in the street. Julia yelled out the window to remind me again to be home for dinner. We would be eating a picnic supper at *Sacre Coeur*, and I had to remember to pick up a *baguette* and some cheese and *paté*.

I walked to the metro *Ternes*, boarded a smelly train, transferred at *Etoile* to the *RER* and got off at *Saint Michel*. Crowded, it was, the *Quartier Saint Michel*. I was early to meet Nadya, so I crouched by the corner of the fountain, just close enough to get some of the water spray on me, and opened the Orangina. There were street performers attracting all kinds of people from God-knows-where. One young man, well-chiseled and muscular, was doing acrobatic moves to the delight of several young, squealing children. Another man of African descent was shouting out a diatribe against the French government's policies in his continent; nobody was really listening, not even the old lady handing out religious tracts trying to shout above him. Three policemen were standing around a homeless man with greasy blond hair just in front of me asking him questions he did not understand. A third performer with long black dreadlocks, rips in his jeans, and a sun-faded guitar sat at the other corner of the fountain playing a dirge in English. I stood up to focus. I could only make out some of the lyrics, but they went something like this:

When you only got pennies, nickles, and doimes, you only got friends some of the toimes. But when you got ones, fives, and tens, then brother, you got friends.

Interesting. Must be the American perspective of life I had long forgotten during my stay in the City of Lights. What was I going back to in the U.S.A. anyway? Dismal capitalism? What did Julia and I actually stand to gain by going back? Couldn't we make a go of it a bit longer here in Paris? Did I really need to get back to my family and the problems they offered? I suddenly got very sullen.

'Michael!' a voiced shouted out over the din of the crowd. It was Nadya, marching across the plaza to where I was sitting. Close behind her was P.G., wearing a tight Speedo bathing suit, white sneakers, and a salmon-colored tank-top.

Nadya came up to me and kissed me on both cheeks. 'P.G. wanted to say goodbye to you, so I brought him with me. Where's Olivier?'

I didn't answer her. 'Good to see you, P.G.' I pointed at his Speedo and laughed. 'Looks like you're smuggling grapes.'

'It's a dandy sunny day,' said P.G. 'So you're leaving this Gawd-awful city and returning to Washington, D.C.' He grabbed the Orangina out of my hand and sucked it down.

I nodded.

'Can I have your address?' he said, handing me the empty can. 'In case I ever make it back to the States, though the FBI is probably still after me for those court problems in Florida I went though.'

I pulled out my wallet and handed him my card with my post office box address on it. 'Write me and let me know when you are coming. You are always welcome to stay with my Julia and I. But you can't wear that banana hammock in the U.S. of A., or they will think you are a poof.'

'Swell. Group hug?'

'P.G., you and I have been hugging all morning,' said Nadya. 'Why don't you go to the gym and pump yourself?'

'Ah. I can take a hint. Michael, we only just met a few months ago, but I feel as if I have known you since Moby Dick… was just a smelt. Please keep in touch.'

'I will. Take care of yourself, P.G.,' I said.

P.G. started to jog in place, and after a few moments he waved a hand and took off on a leisurely run up the *Boulevard Saint Michel*.

Nadya looked sad as she stood there, leaning slightly forward and holding her stomach. 'Is something wrong?' I asked.

'Let's walk,' she said. So I followed her lead, and we headed towards the Seine.

We ambled by an old toothless bookseller next to the *quai*. I stopped to rifle through the stacks, but Nadya grabbed me by the arm and pulled me forward. When we made it to the *Pont Neuf*, Nadya started across at a much slower pace. I could tell she had much on her mind that day. Midway across she stopped and leaned back against the stone wall. I pulled my camera from my courior bag and snapped a picture of her in her lovely sun dress. She did not say much then.

We stood there for quite a while in the warm sun on the *Pont Neuf* exchanging pleasantries and watching the fast moving Seine river flow beneath us. It was a sad moment, knowing that I would be leaving in a day and that Nadya and I may never see each other again.

'You know, Michael,' she said. 'I was thinking-'

'Don't hurt yourself.'

'Funny.'

I smiled weakly.

'No seriously. I spent all morning with P.G.,' her head hung low. 'And yes he pays me well. Better than most. But, I was thinking.'

'Go on,' I encouraged.

She looked at me. 'Tell me if you agree. I am gonna quit being an escort and go to university to study fine arts in England as my father wished after I finish my time at The Wall Street Institute. My English is good enough now for university, *non?*' She looked at me for affirmation.

I nodded in agreement. She smiled greatly, grabbed my hand, and looked down at the rushing Seine.

She leaned again over the bridge's railing, resting her free arm on the cold stone. I followed her move.

'It is a good plan for me, but Michael, things may change. I wish my father were here. I need him so much now.'

'You never mentioned your father before,' I said. She released my hand from hers. (I found out later from P.G. that Nadya's diplomat father had been assasinated by a Muslim fascist just a few years earlier in front of the *Galleries Lafayette* on *Boulevard Hausman* right there in plain sight of a large crowd and God. Never did Nadya mention this to me.)

After I said that, we just stood there silent, not wanting to disturb one another's peace, staring down at the Seine.

She put a hand to her stomach. 'Michael, I think I am pregnant.'

I turned to look at her. A smile faded from her face.

'Michael, tell me what you know about Jesus.'

I responded that all I really knew about Jesus was that I unfortunately knew very little about Him. And that I had to accept that or allow myself to go insane like so many others.

She had a look of consternation. 'Then tell me what you know about people.'

'I guess I don't know much of anything about people either,' I said, putting my hand in hers. 'But don't you just gotta love them? I mean – really - aren't people the best part of life?'

The End

The author wishes to thank the following men:

Roy Cook
Todd Sedmak
Will Mahoney
John Stait
Stephen Dugan
Paul McCabe
Leonard Gordon
Dana Gramling
David O. Davis
Robert Brantley

And of course my good homies:

David L. Newman
D. Sean Newman

And lastly, my beautiful son,

Mikito

You all make me a better man.

FREE T-SHIRT CHALLENGE

If you choose to read (or have read) Michael's first published book, *Cocktails In Paris* (ISBN 0-595-38654-7), try to find the fictional-character name hidden as a pun somewhere among the pages. Hint: the character's name is from a J.D. Salinger novel. Once you find the character's name, write it down on a 3x5 card along with the page number where you found the name hidden and your name and address and mail it to the following address:

Name Contest
c/o The SandyBeachBum Company
301 South Jackson Street
Arlington, Virginia 22204

Winners will receive a custom SandyBeachBum T-shirt as a prize. ☺

(Contest open only to original purchaser's of *Cocktails In Paris*.)

Good luck!

A full 100% of the profits from the sales of this book will go to poor children's families in Trujillo, Peru. My wife, Julia, grew up in a poor slum of Trujillo before leaving to come to Paris looking for a better life. Almost 80% of the children in Trujillo live below the international poverty line as established by UNICEF.

On behalf of the children and their families who benefit from your purchasing this book, Julia and I wish to thank you warmly for your support. May God bless you and keep you, lift His Countenance upon you, and bring you peace.

- Michael W. Newman
Michael@TheDrunkenSot.com